THE CROSSOVER

By

Steven MacGregor Cormack

PublishNation
www.publishnation.co.uk

Dedicated to my son, Reid.

Chapter 1

Sitting motionless, Morgan tried to catch his breath. The flickering light above his head beamed the moving picture onto the screen that glared before him. As he sat there he listened intently to the sounds all around. The rustling of popcorn bags, the rattling of straws sucking up soft drinks through ice and the constant whisper that didn't seem to come from anywhere. The cinema itself felt uncomfortably hot and the accompanying acoustics overly loud, but despite this the place was almost full. As for the film? Morgan didn't know nor care. He'd barely glimpsed at the movie that cost him what little money he had left. Gazing over his shoulder he looked up the aisle through the hazy channel of projected blue light to the entrance behind him. Then, every so often, he'd look to the front of the stage where to the right-hand side of the screen a dim green glow marked the emergency exit. Gradually with each minute that passed he became more and more relaxed, but by then the credits were drawing near. When the film ended he hid among the anonymity of the crowd in an attempt to make his escape. He'd plenty of time to get his head together to decide what he should do. It was simple really, as there wasn't too much of a choice. He would go home and rethink the entire situation.

As Morgan twisted the key in the lock of his front door he was reminded he wasn't coming home to a loving wife or girlfriend in his very own home. No, reality hit him like a bucket of icy cold water drenching him in instant truth as it always did when he reached this point. He'd always tried to forget his home life while he was out, and was only ever reminded by the squalid mounds of uncollected bin bags and indescribable levels of putrid waste that had been allowed to accumulate outside. There were many other telltale signs on show besides, each one launching its own lurid assault on the senses. There was the exposed septic tank by the MacBride kid's sand pit next door, the public urinal cubicle generously provided by BT, and the randomly discarded rubber johnny usually found draped somewhere over the hedgerows or kerb at the side of the road. And there was the

1

rusted baby's pram and the freshly laid coil of dog excrement not yet mature enough to incubate fly larvae like its older cousins. The stripped down Ford Cosworth courtesy of the local thieving carjacking junkies and the utter lack of any kind of nature. Even the dubbed 'fun park' at the end of the street was a potential death trap with its steep sided half drained pond of mud which seemed to be more reminiscent of the Californian tar pits than anything else. Not forgetting of course, the obligatory abandoned shopping trolley which in this instance had been skilfully wrapped around the telegraph pole in his own front garden, for many an intolerable eyesore but for those who sculpted it undoubtedly a very important and significant piece of urban modern art. Then there was the nutty old woman from across the street. A.K.A. the 'Cat Woman' who'd turned her home into one giant cat litter tray as a sort of sanctuary to the neighbourhood strays. The resulting smell of cat piss was so unbelievably strong, that like pepper spray or some kind of biological weapon, it seemed to aggravate the skin, eyes and nervous system of any unwitting passerby who got too close. Not that many ever did. At least not anymore. However, such information comes at a cost. Like pioneers to some strange and foreboding land, sacrifices had been made. Casualties if you will, who'd simply never returned from their perilous quest into the unknown. The milkman, postman, paperboy, even an entire team from the RSPCA accompanied by Alan Davies and a BBC film crew to name but a few. The latter coincidentally being the streets only real taste of fame since the Daz Doorstep Challenge failed to get their whites whiter than white. Or when *Ground Force* refused to do Mickey 'wide boy' Maclean's garden on the basis that he was squatting in a condemned tenement high rise. Not to mention that he became 'Queen Barbra Slutcakes' on the weekends and was due to appear on *Crimewatch* that very same week for armed robbery. Perhaps the general state of the place could be best summed up by a leaked report from the local council which deemed the area unworthy to house asylum seekers, claiming instead that they'd be far better off staying in their war torn refugee encampments despite whatever humanitarian disaster was taking place. And sadly they were probably right as this estate and the neighbouring estate would often clash on a Friday night making any scenes from the Middle East look rather tame in comparison. Home sweet home. How could he disown this?

Once safely indoors and free of them all, Morgan quietly attached the small latch lock back onto its chain. He then proceeded to creep his way through the shadows guided only by a small red forty-watt light bulb that flickered almost constantly as it hung from the first-floor landing. He stopped a little way from the foot of the stairs just before a Mr Lucus's door. He'd come to realise that if he held back and waited until the light turned off his chances of an unimpeded passage onward were far greater than if he were to simply carry on regardless. Knowing this he stalled for a moment to remind himself of the vague timing between the lights feebly indecisive blinks. When he was confident or at least half convinced that a pattern had emerged, he readied himself for everything to black out. Then, under the cover of darkness, he made a blind break for his shared flat on the first floor. Suddenly, and without warning, the bulb flashed sending out a short yet unmistakeable pulse of red light. Morgan instinctively stopped dead in his tracks. He could've sworn he'd seen the silhouette of something directly in front of him. Something quite large. Then there was the smell, an almost overwhelming stench like death, only mobile. This alone was enough to persuade Morgan that it wasn't some kind of subliminal mind trick brought on by his own heightened paranoia. He froze and waited for the light's inevitable return. The hair on the back of his neck stood on end and he could feel a cold prickly draft which instantly gave him goose bumps all over. His heart raced then quickly sank as the light revealed his worst fear. It appeared he'd been sprung. For Morgan was now confronted by what can best be described as a royal pain in the ass and his only real nemesis. The landlord! A man so overweight that any hint of gender or age seemed to have been almost completely obliterated by his own spectacular mass of undulating blubber. On the one instance you'd swear that 'It', as Morgan often referred to him, was just a really effeminate man, but on the other he'd look equally like a particularly masculine woman. In both cases he appeared to be aged anything between sixteen and sixty. He was, to coin a phrase, a kind of sexless man-child. Ultimately though he was nothing more than a vile little creature with the facial characteristics of fungus infested cheese boasting all the charisma and wit of a turkey drumstick. He, 'It' whatever you want to call him, didn't even really look of this world but was vaguely humanoid in his attire. Although he certainly didn't appear to be intelligent so therefore seemed incapable of communication. Astonishingly however, this monosyllabic lump of congealed lard spoke, but not before the light faded out once again to leave Morgan and 'It' alone together in the dark.

Then breaking the eerie void of silence, "Ah, there ye are! Ah've been waitin' fir ye. Ya wee chancer. Tryin' tae slip by unnoticed like a sly fart were ye? Never works. Ah can always sniff out the shite! Besides, Ah didnae come down the Clyde in ay banana boat in the last shower ay fuckin' rain, pal," 'It' said, waddling out in front of Morgan to block his path like some kind of demonic guardian troll standing over the gates of hell.

"Jesus fuckin' Christ, Raymond! What ye doin' creepin' around in the shadows? Ah near pished ma pants," Morgan confessed, nearly jumping out of his own skin.

"Oh, Ah'm sorry. Did Ah gee ya a scare? Ya big Jessy! Anyway, now that Ah got ye dae ye know that Ah had some fuckin' crazy foreign whack job snooping around our gaff earlier the day. Coloured guy. Spoutin' some shite about God only knows what. And generally stickin' his nose where it dinnae belong. Said he was lookin' fir Stuart. Which is kinda funny. Especially as Ah specifically told ya that Ah dinnae like tae be disturbed," Raymond continued, his tone of voice strained and his throat gargled with phlegm as he stabbed at Morgan's chest with an accusing finger.

Morgan just wanted to back slowly away as if faced with some kind of predatory animal. "Well, there really is nothin' that Ah can dae about the state ay yer mental health, Ray boy," he then quipped as he took a guarded step back.

"What? Aye, whatever. Anyway, thankfully Ah got rid ay im'," Raymond, declared triumphantly.

"Who?"

"The guy."

"What guy?"

"The guy from outta town!"

4

"Eh… Who? Outta town? What guy from outta town?" Morgan stressed, realising he was still none the wiser.

"What? Ah'm Ah yer personal messenger? Look, it doesnae matter! That's the least ay yer worries. Ah only mentioned that as ay subtle non direct approach tae something far greater. Ah'm ay course referring tae matters ay far mair pressin' importance. Ye might even say outstanding importance. Ye owe me rent. And Ah want it right nou, sunny Jim! Nae mair ifs, buts or maybes," Raymond said turning his attention to Morgan's overdue rent.

"Foreign chap ye say? Now that ye mention…"

"Shut it, you! Rent! Ye know sweet FA. Sae dinnae play games wi me nob-end!"

"Aye, sure thing, Raymond man. The rent. Ah huvnae forgotten. Ah'm on the case. Dude, as far as Ah'm concerned yer as good as paid."

"Well?" Raymond asked impatiently as he rubbed his thumb, index and middle fingers together, employing the internationally recognised gesture for hard cash.

"Well… ye'll have it first thing in the morning. Dinnae ye fret, pal. Now isnae really the best time though. Unless that is ye know whether it's possible tae make a twelve-inch deluxe deep pan pizza wi aw the trimmings out ay single slice ay mouldy white bread, a courtesy sachet ay Macdonald's ketchup, a partially chewed Peperami and half a carton ay curdled milk… Never mind, long story. Can't stop, gotta go," Morgan replied as he attempted to squeeze past Raymond's vast, bulging curry stained belly before the light failed yet again.

Raymond however wasn't going to budge and he certainly wasn't going to be fobbed off by Morgan's lame assurances, at least not this time. "Oh, a dae apologise yer Godliness. Ah didnae mean tae inconvenience ye or nothin'. When dae ye think ye could fit me intae yer hectic celebrity style schedule in that? Cheeky tosser! It would seem that nae time is ay good time as far as yer concerned ya wee tube. And tomorrow ma arse by the way," he then sneered.

"Come on, amigo. A man's gotta eat. An army never marches on an empty stomach after aw. Everybody knows that," Morgan said optimistically.

"Look, fanny fart. Dinnae piss on ma back and tell me it's rainin' or Ah'll be the one goin' tae war in a minute. And the way Ah feel right now ye could starve tae death tryin' tae sook the peanuts outta my shite. Now that may seem a tad harsh, but Ah'm through caring."

"Nae sae much harsh as just plain gross," Morgan interjected.

"Maybe it's just that Ah huvnae been making masel clear tae ye. Sae Ah'll make it crystal! Ah make the rules. No you. In here Ah'm God. And you, well yer nothin' but a daft wee pussbag whose rent is three months overdue. And ya still ain't coughed up any dosh. AH WANT MA FUCKIN' MONEY NOW OR YER OUT! How's that? Ah really hope that's clarified things cos Ah'd hate tae lose my rag and dae somethin' rash like, Ah dunno, eh? Evict ya!" Raymond belched, his furry yellowish complexion turning almost puce with frustration.

"That's beautiful. Charmin' as ever, Ray. Real colourful. Ah mean what a rapier wit. It's kinda like ya paint a picture wi words. But... what exactly are ye tryin' tae say, man? Ah just dinnae follow you at aw. Ah'm sorry. Yer clever subtlety has baffled me. Cos Ah sense there's a message here but, *woooosh!* It's gone right over my heid. Can you no try and be a little less cryptic? Ha, ha, ha! Oh?" Morgan joked nervously but this was hardly the time to volley back any kind of sarcastic wisecracks especially given the unpredictability factor Raymond brought to any meeting. The very fact that he wasn't communicating in his customary dialect (a succession of incoherent animal noises usually in the form of grunts and snorts) was a clear indication that he wasn't going to be more difficult that usual to shake off.

"Ah want ma money, clever dick! Or Ah'm gonna rip these off and flush em' doon the bog. Simple," Raymond said softly as he reached sharply down to grab an unforgiving hold upon Morgan's unguarded testicles.

"AHHHH! IYAHHHA! OWAHHH! NOOOO! AHHHH, OKAY! STOP! PLEASE STOP! AHHHH! IYAHHHA! SWEET JESUS! OKAY! MERCY GODDAMN IT! MERCY!" Morgan squealed as he squirmed around like some kind of snared animal.

"It's almost like havin' the *Bee Gees* playin' live just for me. Ay course, Ah hate the soddin' *Bee Gees*. Fuckin' screeching freaky toothed buffties. But there's nae denyin' ye got the whole womanly wail down tae a tee. Aye, ye know yer really quite a talented lad. Ya should try out for that *Pop Idol* reality T.V. show pish," Raymond said, toying ruthlessly with his prey.

"Ahh, ahh, ahh, iyahh! Ah always knew there was a comedian inside you fighting tae get out. That's what Ah love about ya. Yer a funny guy. And a passionate understanding kinda guy. And did Ah mention how handsome and suave yer lookin' the night. Ah almost mistook ye fir, eh?... Sean Connery," Morgan said grovelling unashamedly and with more than adequate reason.

"Yeah, yeah, yeah. Sae what are ye gonna dae, punk?" Raymond asked, easing his ball crunching hold on Morgan.

"Well, Ah dunno why ye didnae just say? Dinnae stress out or nothin'. Ah'll nip upstairs and get the rest ay the money from Stuart and we'll be well and truly sorted. Okay?" Morgan murmured in a desperate attempt to appease him but wasn't altogether sure if his message had penetrated.

"Hmmm, cornflakes," Raymond dribbled as he chewed out and ate the dirt from under his fingernails now seeming unaware of Morgan's presence, but more importantly relinquishing his grasp on his particulars.

Nonetheless, this response confused Morgan for a moment as it didn't seem to have much bearing or relevance to anything. "Eh? Rooster? Cereal? Err? Mornings? Hello, Ray? Does attention deficiency disorder mean anything tae ya?" he then asked believing he'd failed to crack Raymond's erratically surreal train of thought.

"What the hell jive are ya talkin' about ye drug obsessed bampot? This isnae some kinda word association game we're playin' here. Ah'm just feelin' a little peckish, alright?" Raymond explained snapping out of his cornflake induced trance.

"And ya always have a silvery string ay saliva hangin' from yer lower lip when ye think ay food dae ya? Ye manky shite. Go on wipe it off. That's truly minging, man. Quite frankly ya look 'special,' dude. Although, Ah must confess that it's very you. Ah mean it finishes off yer ensemble perfectly."

"Ah think Ah've had just about enough of yer cheeky, lip smart arse. Besides, Ah'm missin' ma favourite programmes cos ay you.

MONEY. FETCH. NOW!" Raymond spat out, each word carried through the air by a smell, an unpinpointed odour the closest Morgan believed to be rotting fish, cigarettes and some kind of vinegar or cheap stale French beer.

Disappearing upstairs Morgan dashed around the flat frantically trying to make up the cash to pay their now not so patient landlord. It seemed as if his little payment dodge had finally come to an end. The threat of an eviction notice had seen to that and this time Morgan knew it was for real.

"Stuart! Where the hell is yer half of the rent money? 'It' wants it. Ah mean he's pissed. Ah've never seen 'im like this before. He really wants us tae square up or we could very well end up destitute wi nae roof over our heids," Morgan gasped, able to breath free from the acidic cocktail of poisonous gas that made up Raymond.

Stuart was in his usual outstretched position on the couch. He did as little as possible and if he did do something or make any kind of definite movement it was only through absolute necessity. In other words, if Morgan was out and he wanted something to eat, to go to the toilet, to get off the couch to go to bed or worst-case scenario, fire! Basically, only if his lifestyle was threatened in some way.

"Eh? Who-in-the-where-and-what-now? Ah ain't prostituting masel for naebody!" Stuart slurred, coming to and pulling the hair away from his startled and bewildered eyes.

"What?" asked Morgan baffled by Stuart's gibberish.

"Okay, well how much are we talkin' about exactly?"

"Err? No! Destitute, homeless, without fixed abode. Ye stupid bastard! Ah couldnae gee you away. No that ye could score in a barrel full ay fanny anyway. Look, please just tell me if ye have the cash sae Ah can get this over and done wi and get that clatty fat prick off ma back," Morgan pleaded.

"What?" Stuart asked, now totally confused.

"Yer half ay the fuckin' rent!"

"Eh? Troosers. It's in ma troosers, pal. Just hold yer horses." Stuart yawned, still half asleep, but then that was him fully awake.

"Brilliant, where are yer troosers?" Morgan asked hurriedly, desperate to get back downstairs to resolve this nightmare situation or buy them a little more time at the very least.

"Well, Ah'm bloody wearing em', ya twat. What dae ye think? Ah dinnae make a habit ay walking around raw bollock naked ye know. One tends tae get arrested for that kinda thing. Although, Ah will acknowledge that Ah'm depriving the world ay quite the wondrous spectacle. Or should that be spectacles?" Stuart chuckled as he reached into his pocket and produced his half.

Morgan, more than a little stunned by the speed of Stuart's cash transaction, was momentarily distracted by something equally disturbing. "Hardy fuckin' har. And aye, if only that was true. Ah seem tae remember no sae long ago you being cautioned by the polis for dancin' starkers through the streets wi a traffic cone on yer heid while very much under the influence. And singing the Rod Stewart hit, 'Dae ye think Ah'm sexy'? And no, it wasnae in the least bit sexy. And WOW! Oooh, ma God! What is aw that pish ye've scribbled on the walls for Christ's sake? If Raymond see's that flipping mess he'll go ballistic! He's looking for just that sort ay thing as an excuse tae kick us out. Anybody would think that ye were deliberately tryin' tae sabotage ma life, ya gremlin shite," he then said pointing to their newly decorated walls.

"What dae ye mean 'scribbling'? Art! It's art ye uncultured fuck! A mural tae be exact. Like graffiti, only mair classy. Fair brightens the place up dinnae ye think? My sixth form art teacher always said that Ah was the highly artistic type. Ye know Ah never realised what a Palestine ye were Morgan," Stuart explained, defending his artistic integrity.

"Philistine, Stuart, philistine. And Ah think ye'll find that's highly autistic type. And if yer no frantically cleaning this place when Ah return Ah swear that Ah won't be held responsible for ma actions. There'll be murder on the streets ay Glasgow the night," Morgan warned Stuart with a disgruntled sigh as he made his way back downstairs to give Raymond his rent.

"It took ya long enough! Just goes tae show what a little incentive can dae. But dinnae be late again. Oh and eh, Ah'll be around sometime this week for a wee gander at upstairs. Just tae make sure yer nae trashing the place like ya student types are want tae dae, ye understand. Aye, that's right. A surprise inspection. Ye willnae know when. Could be the night, tomorra or later in the week. Who knows?

9

But it will happen. Cos Ah'm on tae ya. Aye, the day ay reckoning is at hand. Ye worthless gobshite! And Ah for one cannae wait," Raymond revealed as he quickly took the money from Morgan.

Morgan promptly shrugged his shoulders as if this wasn't a potentially major problem especially taking into account Stuart's new found creative outlet. It was as if he somehow knew. "Oh perfect. Ah was just speakin' tae Stuart about that very thing. Ye must be psychic. No that it's any bother tae me, ay course. Ambush away, ma good man... Wait, Ah'm sorry. Ma fault. Ah wasnae payin' close enough attention. What a donut. When exactly did ya say that inspection was again? Ah swear Ah'd lose ma heid if it wasnae screwed on," he said, knowing full well that Raymond would be totally preoccupied counting his money.

"Here's a free piece ay advice. Pull yer heid outta yer arse cos ye'll nae find the light switch in there. Ah dunno? Tomorra, sometime after lunch let's say," Raymond answered, giving up his secret plan with remarkable ease.

"Tomorra? Really? Well, Ah hope that ya dinnae catch us out. That would be embarrassin'. No tae mention worryin' that ma student lifestyle is havin' such a devastatin' effect on ma short-term memory," Morgan confessed.

"Oh, Ah'll get ya. Now beat it before ya have tae have ma foot surgically removed from yer arse. Oh, and next time that Ah see ya Ah want the rest ay yer rent, okay? This is barely fuckin' half! Ah'm considering this tae be a down payment. Oh, and one more thing by the way..."

"What?"

"Replace that stupid red light up there. It's on the blink. No tae mention it makes it feel like a damned whorehouse out here," Raymond grumbled, gesticulating towards the offending light bulb blissfully unaware that he'd blown his chance to catch them off guard.

On Morgan's return he firmly closed and bolted their front door. This was purely a precautionary measure and their first and only real line of defence against Raymond's rather disturbing tendency for nude sleepwalking. Stuart on the other hand was sitting bolt upright on the couch by this time, and by the looks of the flat had made absolutely no attempt at clearing the floor of beer bottles and empty carry out containers. Morgan, clearly agitated by this, launched himself at Stuart grabbing him around the neck. But neither had the energy for the follow up struggle.

"If Ah wasnae sae physically drained Ah'd give ya a damn good paggerin'. Why are ya such a bone idol bastard? Aw ya ever seem tae dae is sit on this couch aw day watchin' Australian soaps and gettin' stoned off the old wacky tobacky. Is it any goddamned wonder that yer beginning tae sound like a bad actin' Australian? Yer about as much use tae me as a box ay waterproof teabags," Morgan said, opting instead for the less energy consuming verbal assault. But even that seemed exhausting.

Stuart just able to deflect Morgan's unexpected lunge attack looked visibly startled by his sudden reappearance. "Hey, man! Ah could've kicked yer arse fir that. Catch me by surprise at the wrong time an Ah could snap yer neck in an instant. Ye'd be deid before ya hit the deck. It's a reflex action. It's aw in ma ninja like trainin'. Cos that's what happens when you upset the natural balance and rhythm ay a finally tuned instrument ay death such as masel. And dinnae speak tae me about useless things. That solar powered torch ya gave me is a complete joke."

"Ah know and a pretty poor one. Anyway, balance and rhythm? Reflex action? Ninja like trainin'? What the bloody hell are ya talkin' about? And yer eyes. Jesus Christ, can you even see? Ah swear ya'd put Christopher Lee tae shame wi those things. That's some scary shit right there. Ah mean, does the Fraggle runnin' the controls in yer heid no get affected by yer drug intake?" Morgan asked, shaking his head as he peered into Stuart's wasted and bloodshot eyes.

"Ma personal vibe, man, is what Ah'm talkin' about. Ya messed up ma shit. What is wrong wi you anyway? Cos ma unthreatening desire tae smoke weed has never bothered ya before now. Was the pizza place closed? Is that it? And just where in the flyin' fuck did ye emerge from aw ay sudden anyway? Ye sneaky bastard. Ah near shat masel," Stuart asked, unconvinced that he was the sole contributor and reason for Morgan's foul mood.

11

"Fuck's sake, Ah was just here no two minutes ago, remember?" Morgan despaired.

"Remember what?"

"Me being here two minutes ago for cryin' out loud! For the rent?"

"Ye've lost me. Ah dunno? Was Ah there? Wait, that actually happened? Ah thought Ah was dreamin'."

"Oh my God! It would appear that ye weren't there then, and ya ain't here now... And look at the state ay this place. That's what's wrong. The front door cannae open and close properly there's sae much rubbish strewn about. And as for yer pizza? Well, ya have nae inkling ay the dangers that lie just outside that front door. Ah was very nearly ripped apart tryin' tae get us food tonight," Morgan informed Stuart as he collapsed onto the sofa beside him.

Stuart's eyes picked up in intrigue but only marginally. "Oh aye! How so? And just where the hell is ma pizza, ya radge? Cos Ah got the munchies in a bad way, man. Ye better no have eaten it ye flabby streak ay pish. What a selfish dick. And ye have the nerve tae bad mouth me."

"Well then, Ah can assure ye, Ah dinnae forget. And if Ah had scoffed it Ah would've been perfectly within ma rights tae. After aw, Ah got it and Ah paid for it and Ah..."

"Right, sound. Now shut yer cakehole, fatty. Here, dae ya want a blast ay Mary Jane? Ah'm pretty baked masel, enjoy," Stuart said, interrupting to offer Morgan a joint.

"Oh! Mr Ah'll state-the-blatantly-bloody-obvious. Ah'm glad tae know that ye've had such ay productive day," Morgan groaned sarcastically.

"Well, ma mate Roach got me a shit-hot deal on some home grown skunk. Tax free ay course. And it's fuckin' wicked, man. Ah just couldnae let it slip by without sampling it like. Where dae ye think Ah got the money that Ah gave ya for the rent? Should make a tidy wee profit off it tae. Go on, man. Smoke that bad boy. It'll send ye intae another dimension. Sae better go steady actually. Ye dinnae wanna go and whitey. Nobody wants tae come across like ay rank amateur. Ah dinnae care who ya are that's just plain embarrassing." Stuart explained as Morgan exhaled his first puff.

12

"Wow! That is strong... feel kinda... like Ah might actually..." Morgan admitted, the whole room now seemingly morphing and spilling over him like some strange warm liquid blanket.

"Hello, Morgan?" Stuart asked as Morgan sunk a little deeper into the couch.

"... Aye, eh? Anyway, speakin' ay yer mate Roach, is he outta here yet? That deranged Welsh arsehole is the reason we have nae food. That and the fact that the process ay decay seems tae have been magnified ten fold in here. At least ya made a wee bit cash out ay it Ah suppose. Although, Ah wish you'd gee a proper job. Dealing drugs isnae exactly a great career choice. And that's before ya get intae the legal ramifications. Any-bloody-way, dae ye want tae hear the craic ay what happened tae me the night or no?" Morgan asked, before getting back to his original train of thought.

"Okay, yer askin' tae questions there. 'A', yes he's gone. And 'B', no particularly ye whingeing fanny."

"Right. Well, Ah did buy a pizza and was in fact on ma way back here when Ah passed by Fat Tam's scrapyard. And there it was. Ma motorbike and sidecar just sitting there. Practically beggin' me tae save it. Ya beauty, Ah thought."

"Oh, good Lord. No this carry on again, man. Are we really havin' this conversation?"

"Sae anyway, Ah decided tae nick it back. After aw, it is mine. Unfortunately, the gate was barely open when these tae massive hairy black bastards appeared and came runnin' toward me like."

"Fuck! Nae the 'Hard Nut' brothers?" Stuart interrupted.

"Who? No, ya stupid dick! Tae friggin' Doberman. Sae Ah legged it. Shitein' masel wi every step. Ah was forced tae lob the pizza at them in the desperate hope they'd eat it and no me. But they had their sights firmly fixed on ma arse. In the end Ah reached that little cinema on the corner sae Ah used ma last five quid tae hide in there. Ah felt pretty confident that they were gonna follow me in. What a pisser ay a day. Aw that for a pizza which Ah didnae even get the chance tae smell, never mind taste. Yet if that wasnae enough tae deal wi, Ah end up face tae face wi our lovin' landlord. That repugnant, hairy shouldered little puke pervert in a stinkin' string vest that we hate sae much. Ah'd rather shag Jabba the Hut than that

13

sack ay detritus. And Ah'll tell ye this anaw. If ya could take life back tae the store, Ah'd get a refund. And then Ah'd march straight up tae God's office and Ah'd say, 'hey, looky here, yer aw fuckin' mightiness, just cos Adam and Eve fucked up dinnae bring it out on the rest ay us. Alreet, pal?' And Ah'd probably malky the nobber just sae that he didnae forget it," Morgan ranted as he cast a dismissive eye over the day's regrettable events.

"Wow! What? Wait, back this shit up a sec. Ye lost our pizza? In fact no, ya just threw it away? Feeding it tae a mangy dog... Gimme that!" Stuart confirmed before whipping the joint back out of Morgan's weary hand.

"Dog? Dogs. Tae. It's plural. There was mair than fuckin' one. No that one wouldnae huv been enough. And Ah bartered that pizza in exchange for ma life Ah'll have ya know. They were gonna kill me! They're on the loose as we speak. Probably mauling some poor bugger. And they ain't just mangy dogs either. They're mair like vicious steroid injected super dogs wi the taste for human flesh. Like Lassie, only not. His evil clones maybe. If it wasnae for ma decisive quick thinkin' and ingenuity, Ah'd probably be deid. Ripped limb from limb like one ay them antelope chats in yon wildlife programme from off the telly."

"Dinnae believe everything ye see. It's no real."

"What do you mean, no real? It's fuckin' nature, man. Of course it's real, ye daft eejit."

"No, Ah mean they stage it sae they can get the right shot in that."

"It still happens."

"Aye, but it's no very likely tae happen here in the centre ay Glasgow now is it? What a drama queen.... God, what a major bummer. Dae ya know what this means? It means, ma friend, that ma drug induced appetite isnae going tae be appeased. Ye could ay at least have got me some popcorn, ye stingy git. Shit, man, this room is goin' tae be ma coffin! Ah huvnae eaten a decent meal n' two weeks. Ah'm totally Hank Marvin. Ah could eat the proverbial scabby heided wain nae bother."

14

"A slight exaggeration, me thinks. If it was two weeks ye'd be deid. Yer confusing that wi a shower," Morgan giggled as he corrected Stuart.

"Shut yer piehole! Ah'm no the one who lost our supper cos Ah was tryin' tae chore back some crappy clapped out nerd mobile. Oh, well Ah'm probably in danger ay tryin' tae sound positive. And believe me, that's some feat when yer hair is starting tae fall out due tae malnutrition. But Ah'll ask it anyway. Was the film much cop? What was it anyway?" Stuart asked in an attempt to put the whole pizza debacle behind him.

"Eh? *Die Hard 7*. Die till ye be deid. Brilliant. Willis knows the score alright. Terrorist fuckin' bad guys. Nae chance," Morgan then lied.

"Sweet. I've been lookin' forward tae that one… Hold on. That film's no even out yet. Ah just read a preview in ma magazine that says just that. In fact, Ah have it right here. Ah'll just find the page… Here we go. He says, the critic, and Ah'm paraphrasing, Bla, bla, bla, dirty white vest, submachine gun. Ah, there it is. 'Coming tae a cinema near ya soon'. Sae this film isnae even out yet. Ye couldnae have watched it. Someone's tellin' porky pies."

"Okay, it was *The Little Mermaid*. But it's no as if Ah had much ay choice. It's hard tae make an informed decision when yer being pursued by a pack ay wild animals. Besides, Ariel would give anyone the horn."

"Pack ay wild animals? Honestly. What a gay boy. But sure, you may have a point there about Ariel. That said, Disney consistently fails tae deliver on even just a little nudity. Ah mean, why gae her such a great rack and no show it? It's like those seashells are welded on. The tormenting bastards and their goddamned mind games. Ah cannae handle it."

"They're nae doing it tae spite ye. It's a cartoon. For kids. It's no porn, ye dirty little pervert. It's just one ya they things. Ye gotta let this obsession go. And get over it. Cos you keep playin' wi yersel the way ye've being doin' and ye'll wear it down tae the nub. Although, Jessica Rabbit from *Who Framed Roger Rabbit?* Need Ah say mair?" Morgan nodded with a wink.

"Ah know, but it's just sae disappointing. And yer right. It's almost like the first time Ah saw *Great Expectations*. Ah built it up in ma mind tae be the greatest movie ever made, but it wasnae at aw what Ah hoped it'd be. Then what about *The Great Escape*? Spoiler alert. They aw got recaptured or shot. Where's *The Great Escape* in that? Or *The Neverending Story*. A blatantly misleading movie title if ever there was one. And the very fact that there's a sequel in *The Neverending Story 2* just adds insult tae injury. They're no even trying tae hide it. Anyway, it couldnae have been that bad. At least ye got tae go tae the pictures."

"Sae what have ye been up tae, 'Mr international man ya mystery'?"

"Nothin'. Although, Ah did have a really wicked dream about how cool it'd be tae be that guy *Manimal*," Stuart revealed.

"What a fascinating insight intae yer day. And what are ye drivelling on about anyway? Was he no the one from the *Muppets*? The heidcase that was always munchin' cookies. Why would ye wanna be a Muppet? Unless ye like the idea ay having someone's hand firmly wedged up yer ringer."

"No, man. Yer thinkin' ay Animal. The nutter on drums. The one that ate aw the cookies is called, eh? Cookie Monster funnily enough. And they were from totally different shows. No that they were totally different shows if yer know what Ah mean? Animal was a puppet from the *Muppets* and Cookie Monster was a puppet from *Seasamy Street*. Although, Ah think they were both Jim Henson deals. Ah'm no totally sure. Ah may need tae Google that one," Stuart digressed.

"Dinnae bother."

"Anyway, Ah'm talking about *Manimal*," Stuart said, getting back to his original thought.

"Yer gonna have tae throw me a line here, dude."

"*Manimal*, man."

"You repeatedly saying *Manimal* isnae helping."

"Half man. Half animal. Yer never saw it?"

"Ma lack ay knowledge on the subject would indicate that, aye. But clever name. Ah mean, ye've got this idea for a T.V. show about a half man, half animal. But what dae ye call it? Hmmm? Gee, now there's a heid mincer. How long dae yer think they spent twiddling their thumbs before they came up with that brainwave?"

"Man-animal? *Manimal*. Oh aye. Ah mean, aye, that's right. It was a shite show but Ah remembered it being fuckin' class back in the day. Some things are best left tae memory Ah guess, like *Street Hawk*, *Airwolf* and fuckin' *MacGyver*. But anyway, this guy could metamorphous intae a black panther, a black snake, spider or hawk at will. In fact, Ah think he could change intae a bear anaw."

"Which Ah suppose could be surprisingly handy in absurd situations where it would be better tae be a snake, panther, hawk, spider or bear. Aye, some things are definitely best left tae memory. And some might say yersel." Morgan yawned.

"Ah dinnae know. Ah just thought it would be pretty cool," Stuart said, surprised at the lack of interest in his chosen subject matter.

"Yer a right sad wanker, ye know that? It's like each day ye regress a little further. Ye'll be fully retarded by the end ay the week."

"Better than yer story! But alright, 'Mr know it aw'. Here's an interesting fact for ya that Ah read outta that, eh?"

"Book." Morgan sighed before continuing, "Ah dunno what's more ay a surprise. The fact ye can read or the fact Ah'm still listening tae this pish? And at least ma story was grounded firmly on reality, no on some weird unoriginal dream based on a shitty forgotten eighties T.V. show. Where would ye be without the satellite telly and dodgy DVD box sets?" Morgan grimaced as he waited for Stuart's next earth shattering piece of trivial nonsense.

"Aye, fine. But this will twist yer melon. Did ye know that we, Ah mean us humans, only use an average ten percent ay our brains? Madness, eh?"

"That's no sae hard tae believe."

"Sure, but can ye imagine what we would be capable ay if we could just somehow just tap intae the other eighty percent? Some reckon telepathy or perhaps even telekinesis. We'd aw be X-Men! How awesome would that be by the way?" Stuart reasoned.

"We wouldnae be mathematicians, that's for sure. Ye've lost ten percent. And the only thing Ah'm sensing here is bullshit... doesnae matter. Right, well that about sums up ma day. Ah'm going tae ma bed."

"Fine. Piss off then. See if Ah care. Yer shite craic anyway...WAIT! HOLY SHITE! DINNAE AH NO TELL YA YET? Stuart then yelled out, suddenly erupting up off his seat.

"Tell me what? And please, yer scaring me. Wait, it's not going tae be that whole, 'if Ah got blasted by radiation in some freak accident would Ah inherit superpowers' thing again is it? Ye'll never be Spiderman or a member ay The Fantastic Four. We've had radioactive leaks aw over the world and no once have we even had a three-eyed dog, let alone a Godzilla type creature. A horrible, slow and painful death as ay result ay cancer, yes. Teenage Mutant Ninja Hero Turtles, no," Morgan said realising that he'd never seen Stuart move with anything like that kind of speed before.

"No, it's no that. Oh ma God. This is amazing. Ah cannae believe ye dinnae know!" Stuart said, his whole body trembling in anticipation.

"Know what? And chill. Yer havin' a minor fit or spasm. Either that or ye should go tae the bog before ye have an embarrassing accident."

"This is phenomenal! Wait till Ah tell ya! This is gonna blow yer mind!"

"Tell me what?"

"Just what the fuck have we been worrying about?"

"A dinnae know. Where dae Ah begin?" Morgan asked, totally clueless as to what Stuart was getting so wound up about."

"Man, dae Ah feel good tae get that off ma chest. It's like a weight has been lifted from ma shoulders."

"Stuart! Ah have nae idea what yer banging on about. None whatsoever. Ye dae realise that?"

"Have ye no been listening?"

"Listening tae what exactly? Ye've told me sweet fuck aw!"

"Oh right. Ah'm just sae psyched. WE FUCKIN' WON!"

"Won? What? A fish? A cuddly toy? A holiday tae Euro Disney? What?"

"Okay, promise tae stay cool!"

"Ye first! And this better be good."

"It's way beyond good! Something incredible happened while ye were gone, man."

"Well, Ah sincerely hope so. Otherwise ye've got nothin' tae tell me and this has been a huge waste ay ma time." Morgan sighed.

"AH WON THE LOTTERY, MORGAN! Is that far out or what? It's totally wild! Come on, let's celebrate."

"Lottery? Lottery?" Morgan echoed, stunned at Stuart's unfathomable declaration.

"Dinnae worry, Ah could scarcely get over it masel!" Stuart said, jumping up and down in triumph as if he'd just scored The World Cup winning goal for Scotland. (Don't laugh too hard. It could happen. Maybe, okay maybe not. But we live in hope. Sad, pathetic, delusional hope.)

"Yet somehow ye did. Enough tae totally forget. And isnae that something tae just slip intae conversation. What, are ya mental? Oh, and ye'd wait till now after ma night ay living hell tae tell me. Ye didnae win sae there's nothin' tae celebrate. And even if ye did, we got shite aw tae celebrate with. Unless, a half-eaten packet ay Scampi Fries and a carton ay Um-Bongo is yer idea ay a party," Morgan scoffed in instant dismissal.

"Ah just remembered… But Ah did. Really."

"Just remembered? What kinda excuse is that? That's nae something ye forget. Ah very much doubt that it's a forgettable experience. And yet ya managed tae remember that unmitigated obscure shite about *Manimal* or whatever the fuck it was. How the bloody hell dae ye go about forgetting about winning the lottery, ye daft nob? Ye never. Simple as that. Ye've smoked yer tiny skull back tae the Stone Age. God, ye probably dreamt it. Lottery, ya really are gettin' desperate."

"Believe it, man. Ah dunno? Maybe Ah was a wee bit high before. But this isnae bullshite."

"Ah'm sorry. Ah just dinnae believe ye. Why would Ah? Yer sleverin' total pish. And Ah ain't fallin' for it. April Fools passed by months ago. Besides, Ah ain't that gullible."

"Aye, ha, ha, ha, very funny. Sae are ye with me or no? Look, Ah know how it sounds. Ah think Ah'm crazy?"

"Ah dinnae think yer crazy. Deluded. A lying wee toerag or just plain stupid, aye. But crazy, no. It's nae yer fault, ya poor wee sod. Ye can take some consolation in the fact that's what happens when two cousins get it on. Ah mean, Ah assume yer parents were related in some way. It's a recipe for making defective bairns, fella."

"Fuck off!"

"Look, Ah just dinnae believe for one second that today could be totally redeemed by something as utterly and unbelievably cool as becoming a millionaire."

"WELL AH DID!" Stuart stated excitedly, undeterred by Morgan's utter lack of enthusiasm.

"Ay course ya did. And Ah can see the fairies at the bottom of the garden in aw. Tell me, Ah'm curious, but what colour is the sky in the world ye live in?" Morgan said, getting up and dancing from one foot to the other.

"AH DID! AH'M TELLIN' YE! HONEST TAE FUCKIN' GOD!"

"Aye, did ya bollocks! And guess what? Ah solved world hunger, disease, poverty and famine, yet still found time on the side tae help in the struggle for world peace while promoting love on earth. No tae mention publicising my new album and latest fashion range. Cos, did Ah no tell ya? Ah'm the utopian pop star Bono. Oh, and look at that. Ah've just got a text message from ma best pal Bob Geldof askin' me out tae lunch wi Nelson fuckin' Mandela," mocked Morgan.

"Dinnae fuckin' well patronise me! Ya oughta be kissing ma hairy bean bag! Ah'm a millionaire now, man!"

"Aye, course ya are. It aw makes perfect sense tae me now. Ah believe ya. Whatever ya say, Stuart, Ya fuckin' weirdo," Morgan continued. He just wasn't biting.

Chapter 2

Just below Morgan and Stuart 'It' the landlord was sitting down to watch *Wheel of Fortune*. In doing so he'd left his cornflakes to go soggy and decided instead to trim some of the length from his toenails. As he sat there hacking away at their huge, curling banana shape, he tried to predict where the clanking needle would land. As the fluorescent wheel spun ever faster it's bright sparkling colours seemed to dazzle him into an almost hypnotic trance. He spent most of his time watching television but this was by far the highlight of his day. Even more so than the likes of *Diagnosis Murder* or *Jerry Springer* which came a close second and third respectively. One by one he snapped off his nails which spun through the air unpredictably like tiny smelly brown Perspex boomerangs landing all over the floor. Despite this obvious fundamental lack of personal hygiene his flat was reasonably tidy. He was without a shadow of a doubt the filthiest object in the room. Watching the flashing neon screen he cut off the last sizeable chunk of nail which ricocheted off an empty beer tin and planted itself snugly in his bowl of mushy cereal. When Raymond had finished he sat back with his slops and began to spoon it into his cavernous decaying mouth. In doing so he ate the razor-edged piece of nail which embedded itself in his throat. At first, for a second or two, he didn't notice, but when he went to swallow he began to choke violently. The bowl fell to the floor as his hands rose up to clutch at his neck. Tears rolled down his blood swollen face as he squirmed and writhed around unable to shout out for help. A yellow paste of chewed cornflake fell from his flared nostrils while his bulging nicotine stained eyes had never looked more awake. Until eventually he stopped. Dead!

"Okay, wise guy, show me the ticket!" Morgan commanded with outstretched hand.

"Ah cannae. It's nae here."

"Ye mean tae tell me ye've no even got a ticket? Christ, ya need a ticket. Ah reckon there's a fair chance that it's nestled firmly but

21

neatly up yer bum along wi yer heid." Morgan sighed already tiring of the conversation.

"Well, how the hell should Ah know?"

"Ye'd know if ye'd won, idiot. Look, we could die ay hunger in this rat infested shitehole and aw ye can come up wi is some kind ay drugged up story about winning the lottery."

Stuart was now on a mission to convince Morgan that he wasn't making this all up. "Ma new found uncle in America phoned and we got talkin' about the lottery and that. Just making conversation. Ye know how it is? Anyway, before Ah know it Ah'd given him ma lucky numbers and they came up. Just like that!"

Morgan was at this point quite unable to comprehend just how absurd Stuart was being. "Just like that, eh? Incredible. Hold on. New found uncle? And now ye've apparently won the lottery in the United States ay America? Ah dinnae believe ma fuckin' ears. Ah'm Ah hearing ya right? Have you the slightest idea how much like bullshit this sounds? Ah'm getting' some kinda *déjà vu* here. This kinda reminds me ay the time NASA supposedly got in contact about that astronaut job ya had applied for. Ye dinnae even have a valid licence tae drive a car let alone be trusted wi ay multi-million-dollar space rocket. The only space ye'll ever get lost in is the huge void between yer goddamned dumbass ears."

"Ah tell ya it's true!" Stuart shrieked in delight, and again ignoring Morgan's blatant insults.

"Listen tae me, ya wee turd. Today has been shallow enough without coming home tae yer fairy tales, which Ah will admit is the most creative thing ye've ever come up wi. It certainly beats that holiday tae Narnia ye were sae utterly convinced we'd won. Was it no Bosnia or Croatia somewhere like that? And ye never won that either. Thank fuck. Looked a right dive as Ah remember."

"Can ya no try tae be a little more open-minded, Morgan?"

"Open-minded? Ye must think that Ah've got a gaping great hole in ma heid."

"What will it take tae prove tae ye that?"

"Look me in the eye and tell me that ye havnae been at the Airfix glue again."

"Okay, fine. Ah tried. Ah would've been mair than willin' tae share the money wi ya. But if ya will insist on refusin' tae believe that Ah've just become a millionaire then that's up tae you. Just dinnae expect me tae hang around," Stuart informed Morgan as he pulled on his shoes.

"Why? What are ye talkin' about? And just where the hell are ya goin'?"

"Where Ah'm Ah goin'? Ma numbers come up. Ah'm outta here, man. Besides, Ah broke the telly. Jesus, whatever happened tae Velcro? That stuff was pure deid brilliant!" Stuart said, tying up his laces to the best of his ability.

"Leavin'… the flat? Ya cannae be serious. Ya cannae leave. What about me? Wait, ya bust the telly? How the hell did ya manage that? Ye were throwing stuff at it again, weren't ya? If ya wanna change the channel find the bloody remote and use it like a normal person. Either that or scrape yer pathetic hole off the couch," Morgan stewed, realising there was in fact a more tangible issue to deal with.

Stuart stood up and began to hunt around for his jacket. "Ah used the remote. That's what broke the telly. Oh, and that broke too by the way. Which reminds me. We need batteries. Well, actually we dinnae. No anymore. See, who says Ah dinnae save us money? Anyway, man, yer diverging from the topic in hand. What about you? You dinnae believe."

"Dinnae believe? This ain't Never Never Land yer livin' in here. And you sure as hell ain't no Peter Pan despite yer freaky love for aw things nylon. Sae let's come back down tae earth and rejoin reality for a sec, ye absolute raging bawbag."

"Screw you, man! Ah'm basically a pretty laid-back placid kinda guy. But Ah have a threshold for the amount ay verbal that Ah'm willin' tae take. Mind the Incredible Hulk? That's what the fuck Ah'm talkin' about. Ya dig? Ya know Ah really dunno why Ah'm tryin' sae hard tae convince ya anyway?"

"What are ya sayin'? That yer gonna burst outta yer clothes and turn green. What the fuck kinda analogy is that? And yer only tryin' sae hard tae convince me cos ye cannae dae fuck aw for yersel. No tae mention Ah'm yer only real friend. Ah even Ah think yer a tool.

Ye need me," Morgan said, but instantly regretted it as it sounded way harsher than he'd intended.

"Oh, what's this? A knife in ma back? That must be yours. Arsehole!" Stuart said, as he pulled an imaginary blade from between his shoulder blades.

"Okay, okay. Forget Ah said that. Ya know Ah didnae mean that. Ah'm as open-minded as the next guy. It's just… it's just Ah cannae take another kick in the guts. Ah'm sick ay this. Nobody should have tae irk and crawl their way through life wi nothin' better in sight then way we dae. We're young and these are meant tae be the best days of our lives. But it's no. It's total kack. Life isnae a box ay chocolates. It's a shite sandwich. And we aw have tae queue up, take a big bite, smile and say thank you very much. Well, ya can fuck that for a laugh."

"So am Ah, man. Dealin' small amounts ay marijuana tae yer student mates isnae ma idea ay a great career. Sae Ah wouldnae lie. No about sommit like this."

"Okay, let's say for a moment that Ah'm actually buyin' intae this madness and therefore believe that ya did win. Hypothetically speakin' ay course. Just for fun ya understand. How can you collect the money when yer half a world away?" Morgan asked, humouring Stuart.

Maybe it was the look on Stuart's face or perhaps he was just getting jaded, but Morgan began to entertain Stuart's notion. Half of him wanted to believe his fantastic story, but the other knew he must be on another level of consciousness somewhere, probably fuelled by an extensive and varied diet of narcotics and household cleaning products. Either way, he had to play along as it was most likely his best chance of calming Stuart down and ultimately getting a peaceful night. Besides, Morgan was fairly confident that Stuart would lose interest or would fall asleep before long anyway. At least that was the hope.

"Ah dinnae have a Scooby. But we need tae get over there and pronto. Ye know Ah'm talking yesterday."

"Okay, first things first. Getting tae America is one thing. But time travel? Well, that's a pretty tall order. After all the DeLorean failed its M.O.T. and its flux capacitor is outta weapons grade plutonium."

"Great Scott, Marty!"

"Exactly... Wait, what about yer uncle?"

"Dinnae even think about it. He's probably even more skint that we are."

"Well, that's that then, ain't it? Just our luck. Bloody typical. We're millionaires who cannae even afford tae fly in the cargo hold, never mind first class. Irony sucks the big one. Either that or somebody's havin' a right good laugh at our expense. Right, fuck it. Ah'm off tae ma bed," Morgan concluded.

Stuart was in no mood for this. He, for once, was a man of action. "Well, it's pretty clear tae me what we have tae dae. Dinnae be sae defeatist, Morgan," he then said, unfazed by the impossibility of their situation.

"What? What can we possible dae? We've nae money, Stuart. Besides, this whole thing is bollocks anyway. It's over, man."

"Okay. Number one. We mustnae tell a soul. Number two. We must gather up as much dosh as poss for plane tickets. Number three. Take only what we need tae survive. This will ay course include a map and an assortment ay flavoured Pot Noodle. Lastly, if aw goes tae plan, and Ah personally see no reason why it shouldn't, then we live out the rest of our lives like kings. BOOM! We have a plan."

Morgan looked to the roof in pain. Sadly, Stuart wasn't going to be the brains behind this particular outfit and quite why Morgan was getting himself so caught up in this was a mystery. Even to him. It just shows what happens to the human mind when starved of food and television.

"Because everythin' is just that simple. Well, granted ye are. And may Ah just say what a well-planned plan ya huv there. That said, there are a few minor holes Ah think ya may huv overlooked. Holes big enough for me tae climb through. Oh, and if we dae find oursels in some dire situation havin' tae survive off Pot Noodle, Ah think Ah'd rather eat you. Sae ya've been warned. If yer havin' me on, Ah'll cannibalise yer arse."

"Ahh, man! Ah dinnae understand it. What is yer problem?" Stuart muttered from beneath a sizeable frown.

"God! It's like givin' a monkey a shotgun. He just doesnae get it until its tae late. Okay, please try and follow me on this one. Not tellin' anyone Ah think we can just about manage tae afford. In fact, Ah think it's probably for the best. But as ya clearly huvnae grasped, the tickets we cannae. That is unless such a momentous and wondrous occasion arrives where Ah can pull twenty quid notes clean from ma money makin' rectum. Until then, Ah think Ah'm safe in sayin', the rest ay yer carefully constructed plan becomes void," Morgan said, dismantling Stuart's strategy in an instant.

"Ah thought that Ah had it there. Ah really believed that was a plan Hannibal Smith woulda been proud ay. It was totally coming together. Ah had the cigar ready an everythin'. Come on! There has tae be a way. Think, man, think. This is yer department."

"Look, retardo. This isnae *The A-Team*. And nae amount ay handy bits and pieces aw welded together will change that. Sae nae big fat cigar for ya this time… Wait a sec. Yer uncle bought the ticket. Correct?" Morgan then asked, switching direction midflow.

"Aye."

"Well, surely he could just get the money without us. Then he could buy us some swanky first-class flights. Travel in style. No like the rest ay the scum. The solution is sae simple it was starin' us square in the face. God, it must be the air in here, man. Yer poisoning us. Quick, open a window before we succumb tae the fumes."

Stuart lifted his hands up to cover his face. "Aye, he probably could've, but…"

"Yes, Ah knew it. What dae ya mean? Could've, but? 'But' is never good. But is just the short pause linkin' the good from the soon tae be bad."

"But he's in a wheelchair with a speech impediment," Stuart continued.

Morgan paused for a moment. "Is that aw? God, Ah thought ya were goin' tae tell me he'd died or sommit. Look, he's in a wheelchair and he has a speech problem. It doesnae matter. It's hardly a disaster. Sure it may take him slightly longer and he may huvtae repeat himsel mair than once, but at the end ay the day we

26

still come out rich. Ye know Ah never realised ya were such a bigot. Sae he's a spazz. Big deal. Mair power tae him Ah say."

Stuart looked up at Morgan apprehensively from between the cracks of his fingers. "Ah havnae quite finished. He got the ticket on day release from… from prison. Look, Ah know it sounds bad."

Morgan's gob had never been more smacked. "Yer uncle's a criminal?"

"Aye, Ah know."

"Well, Ah gathered that ye know on the basis that ya told me. It's probably just as well he's in prison. How dae ya know that he wouldnae huv gotten greedy and taken the lot?"

"Look, he didnae huvtae tell us at aw. But he did. And besides, Ah'm his only family," Stuart pointed out.

"Hey, remember it's yer numbers. That entitles ya tae at least half," Morgan reasoned.

"Ah guess."

"Ah'm sorry, Stuart. Ah just cannae believe this is happenin'. Ah mean what does this uncle, slash criminal, ay yers want us tae dae? Has he any more prison releases? How long is he in for anyway?"

Stuart clasped his head in his hands once more. "Questions, questions, questions. Aw Ah know is what he told me. He phoned soundin' really desperate. In fact, he sounded kinda down about the whole thing. Anyway, he just said that he was stuck wi the ticket but he'd think ay sommit."

Morgan sat back down. "Sae would ya be if ya'd just won the lottery in prison. Does he huv any helpful friends? Ah mean, this is aw a bit torturous."

"Ah dinnae think they'd believe him."

Morgan nodded in agreement. "Yeah, Ah had a hard enough time believin' you. No that Ah dae mind. Although, Ah must confess, this whole thing is very elaborate. Even taking intae account yer predisposition for total pish."

"No, that's no quite what Ah was gonna say."

"Go on."

"The situation is more complicated than it may first appear. Ye know the agency that found him?"

"No. But dae carry on."

27

"Well, they told me a little about him. For security and that. Apparently when the polis caught him he did nothin' but lie tae them sae his report reads that he's a compulsive liar and utter fantasist. Allegedly."

Morgan had some difficulty at first taking this new information in. "Ah'm glad Ah heard this late, but nonetheless crucial breaking news before ya dragged ma arse on an utterly pointless trip halfway round the globe. Did ye really no think this was significant? Are ya seriously tryin' tae give me some sorta mental breakdown? Tell me everythin'. Just dinnae tell me what he did tae land himsel in prison. Ah really dinnae think Ah'm ready."

"Uncle Lawrence assures me it wasnae much. More ay an accident come misunderstanding."

Morgan was thoroughly staggered at Stuart's blind faith. "Ah dinnae know what worries me more. The fact that ya seem tae believe him. Ah mean have ya questioned any ay this? Or the ideas Ah'm gettin' in ma heid about what he may ay done. Oh, and tell me this. If he's meant tae be a compulsive liar and utter fantasist, how dae ya know he didnae lie about winning the lottery? He's obviously a total mentalist. Or maybe he just wants someone tae pay his way outta the nick. Yer being played, dude. It's as clear as day. Wake up and smell the coffee."

"Look, he's been honest wi me aw the way. He's admitted tryin' tae rob a bank wi a pretend sawn-off shotgun was a big mistake."

"Armed robbery? Sawn-off shotgun?" Morgan gasped.

"Pretend, sawn-off shotgun."

"Okay, but how's that an accident come misunderstanding?"

"No, the accident come misunderstanding had something tae dae wi the Mafia godfather who's after him. He only stuck up the bank outta desperation."

"Mafia godfather? What the fuck? Enough ay is shite! None ay this sets off alarm bells in yer heid? He's no just a potential criminal whack job. He's a potentially dangerous criminal whack job!"

"What do you mean?"

"Oh ma God. Join the dots, ma friend. Deep down ya know it tae. Even ye ain't that much ay a gimp. Ah mean, Ah get yer wasted. But seriously?"

Stuart's bubble had been well and truly burst. "Aye, what am Ah thinkin'? Yer right. Yer always right. Ah'm sorry. Ah guess Ah just got swept up in the moment. Now that Ah've said aw this out loud it does sound a tad far-fetched," he then said as he left the room leaving Morgan alone on the couch.

"Just a tad. Sorry, this gives me no satisfaction, honestly. Ah really love tae be wrong," Morgan muttered to himself.

Chapter 3

Stone grey walls, metal grey bars, small and confined. There was no way out. The stench of captivity hung heavy in the air. A zoo made to hold the most dangerous of animals. A claustrophobic's nightmare.

Uncle Lawrence was in way over his head and he knew it. He wasn't a hardened criminal, killer, rapist or deranged psychopath. He was just plain old Lawrence 'opportunist' Lowmax. However, things had taken a few turns for the worse.

You see, the problem in trying to rob a bank is that in our modern technological age it has become an extremely difficult task making capture fairly inevitable. It may be a small detail lost on Lawrence but forget what you've seen in the movies. That's all bullshit. Fact. It is a skilled art and therefore almost impossible. It hardly ever happens. Successfully that is. Otherwise more people would do it. Sure, some may try, but nearly all fail. There are a number of factors that can make this kind of work amazingly formidable, ranging from laser alarms to armed security guards and tracking devices, to camera equipment, coded vaults and steel bars. Even the staff and customers it would seem. A 'have a go hero' with a hand cannon is as big a problem to your long-term longevity, if not more unpredictable, and any successful plan relies on cutting down on the unknowns. It's also very important to know exactly what it is you're stealing in the first place. As there is absolutely no point risking life, limb and liberty for a bag full of hot diamonds or fine art without having a way to shift it – a buyer – that just makes things even more complicated. As soon as you bring a third party into the equation you've got trust issues, plans change like the flick of a switch or people simply just leave you high and dry. Honour among thieves? Forget about it. Simplicity is key. Plus, you need contacts, time and you've got to have money in the first instance to finance your little endeavour. Doing things right doesn't come cheap. Lawrence had none of these luxuries. Besides, jobs like this take meticulous planning and are generally executed by real pros.

30

Lawrence had next to no experience. That leaves cold hard cash. So jewellers are out and art galleries are most definitely a no go. So the choice narrows down to banks, convenience stores, gas stations and the like. Banks are dangerous but insured and always have money. Really Lawrence should've been thinking small. A gas station or convenience store, that kind of place, because he wasn't stupid. However, he was greedy and perhaps more importantly he was getting desperate. Not to mention the fact that you're just as likely to be shot down in a convenience store as a bank these days. At least that was Lawrence's rationale. So he opted for a small, sleepy country town bank knowing they'd be far less ready for it than a national bank in a big city. They'd sure as hell have far less security measures, and Lawrence believed most of these defences could be overcome by simply donning a good masquerade. With a disguise nobody can see your true identity while you are at work. The usual item used to cover one's face in such a scenario tends to be some kind of balaclava, ski mask or motorcycle helmet. The problem with wearing any one of those is that people tend to know straight away what it is that you're going to do. This can get you caught on either the way in or out of your intended target. Yet Lawrence believed he'd found the perfect way around this particular conundrum. This was by no means his usual style but his options were limited. You see, Lawrence had been a fairly successful and well regarded make-up artist for the film industry in Hollywood. Sadly, he was also known for his gambling and volatile temper. It was the latter characteristic in particular that lost him said job after he knocked out a very famous and influential director who made sure he'd never work in Tinseltown again. Lawrence was always looking for the quick buck, the get rich quick scheme, and when he hit rock bottom he turned to a life of duplicity and became a con man. Unfortunately, for him he was a better make-up artist than he was a con artist, and he'd just jumped in head first into the shallow end of the pool.

Now the bank he'd singled out didn't have the likes of falling bars or laser traps, but it did have alarms, cameras and being a small bank could potentially have a strong community spirit. The main difficulty would come from entering the bank without looking like he was planning to hit the place, while at the same time concealing his true identity from the cameras. He decided it would be best to use up-to-the-minute techniques. Lawrence's plan was to use his skill with make-up to enter the bank undetected. It would also be to his advantage to let the cameras and staff see his fake face, because after he'd fled the scene the authorities would be looking for someone who, in effect, didn't exist. A phantom if you will. It took some imagination to figure out how to then deal with the staff and customers. What he ideally wanted was to somehow split them up in such a way that he only had to handle a few at one time. His solution was nothing short of total lunacy, but it was such a harebrained idea that there was a chance it would work. Another important element to success is surprise and this was to be the make or break part of his plan. He didn't want to go in guns blazing. It wasn't his style. Anyway, that also tends to draw people's attention or worse still get you a one-way ticket to the morgue. And he most definitely didn't want that. Lawrence would scare the staff and customers in a different way. He would deal with one and then the other. So by first using a novelty tin of joke turd spray and a mouthful of whipped cream he planned to shock the customers into leaving the bank. In doing so he'd be left with just the staff and enough time to grab his loot. At least that was the theory.

So on the day he had a taxi wait for him outside the bank as he'd previously crashed his own car. But we'll get to that later. He also figured he wouldn't be long. It was just a small withdrawal, plain and simple, right?

He entered the bank as planned with his lifelike latex face on. Then, when out of view, he sprayed the fake turd as if it were coming out of his trouser leg bottoms and onto his shoes. He also made sure he was well soaked head to toe in stink bombs which he'd concealed and then broken in his pockets. All he need do then was fill his mouth with whipped cream. Within seconds of joining the end of a queue his strong pungent presence was detected by a family nearby. With this he began to dribble his mouthful of whipped cream. This convinced most people that he was a potentially rabid smelly old drunk who'd just soiled himself and that was enough to get them running for the nearest exit. For others a little extra prompting and persuasion was needed. So he ran about with some of the fake crap

32

on his hands screaming like a madman. As you'd expect they couldn't get out of there fast enough. There's nothing quite like the thought of having human excrement shoved in your face to make you recoil in disgust. It's a universal law of nature that we all share. Lawrence had by then pulled out a sawn-off shotgun from under his coat and the staff who'd been fairly bemused by all the fuss safe behind their glass counters now realised too late what was really going on.

With his bag of money, he fled the bank and threw it into the back of the waiting taxi and in turn leapt into the front passenger side. Job done. Well, not quite. Lawrence's only real mistake had been not telling the taxi driver what was going on. The six foot four angered gorilla of a man took one look at his horrid state and planted his fist firmly in Lawrence's latex face leaving a sizeable impression before ejecting him violently from his cab. In the panic and confusion he stumbled across the road and was knocked over the windscreen of a passing car, the owner of which seeing the condition of his once beautiful classic red sports convertible (which he'd personally painstakingly restored) got out and proceeded to kick the living daylights out of Lawrence. This not only left him bloodied and bruised but also set off a time controlled ink cartridge which exploded leaving him, the irate motorist and his ill-gotten gains covered in fluorescent purple dye. When the police arrived in response to the robbery all they found were two purple men fighting on the ground. Both were arrested on the spot.

Lawrence, however, was taken to hospital where his now mangled and quite frankly terrifying latex mask was recognised from the scene of the crime by a female bank teller getting treatment for shock. After about two months in traction, the judge, taking into account his injuries and just how he'd executed his absurd caper decided to be lenient and half his sentence. But only after he'd undergone a thorough mental evaluation. Lawrence was then taken to prison confined to a wheelchair and stuttering like a lunatic.

Yet all of that hadn't been the beginning of Lawrence's misfortune. No, in fact he was having a real run of it which had started only a week or so prior to his attempted robbery gone wrong. The only reason, or at least the main justification for why he took on the bank, was so he'd have enough money to flee the country. Why? Because of the recently buried Mrs Leony. Mrs Leony being the mother of Rico Leony, an extravagantly rich and powerful drugs baron with heavy connections to the Mob, although he looked and lived more like a film star. This appealed to Lawrence who wasn't stupid enough to rip the Mafia off, and he probably wouldn't have dreamt of doing so if he'd only known. But he saw the opportunity to make a quick buck. His first mistake. So now, unsurprisingly, he found himself fearing for his life. He'd been duping his way into the lives of the rich and famous for months, gaining their trust before taking from them what he could and had been doing so with relative success. In fact, he was casing Mr Leony's residence looking for an angle when he thought he'd been caught red-handed. The mansion had up until that point seemed deserted when suddenly Mr Leony appeared from out of nowhere.

"Are you lost? Can I help you, son? This is private property and you're trespassing. I could have you arrested. By law I could even shoot you!" he boomed as he marched straight over to Lawrence.

Lawrence didn't have long. He needed to think fast. "Shoot me? No, there's no need. Eh? I'm here because, eh? I was sent here by… You know what? I've probably got the wrong address," he stammered as he desperately tried to think up a reason for being there but just came off sounding really vague.

"You're damn straight you got the wrong address, Mister! Wait, I'm sorry. Who did you say sent you?"

"Who sent me? Eh, the… agency? Yeah, the agency sent me," Lawrence then lied.

"The agency? You're the new help then are you? For Leony. Is that correct?" Mr Leony then confirmed as he quizzed Lawrence.

Lawrence paused momentarily, his devilish little mind working overtime. He'd never been one to pass up an opportunity. "Eh? Yes, yes I am. And you, you must be Mr Leon."

"Mr Leony."

"Leony, right. I've heard so much about you. It's a pleasure to finally meet you. Sorry to be caught wandering around like this. It's just that you've such a big and beautiful property. I guess that I got a little lost."

"Really? You're the new butler? I'm sorry, what did you say your name was again? It's just that I was told quite specifically by the agency that they had no one available until Tuesday. And yet here you are. A whole day early. Why is this?" Mr Leony asked as he dabbed the sweat from his brow with a handkerchief.

"It's… Ferrari. My name is Mario Ferrari. And yes, I understand completely. I can only assume that there must've been a mix up somewhere along the line with the dates. Or maybe an opening as the result of a cancellation became available. I know the boss sees you as an important client. They wouldn't have wanted to leave you waiting a day longer then was necessary. After all, you know what they say, 'the early worm' and all that jazz," Lawrence said in a desperate attempt to fit in. His fake moustache on the other hand was not.

"Early worm? I didn't say anything about a worm?"

"No, I meant… You know, when you said. Never mind."

"Relax. I'm fucking with you. I know what you meant."

"Ah, good, cos I'm here now. So whatcha gonna do?" Lawrence then chuckled as he shrugged his shoulders.

"Tell you to fuck off! That's what I'd normally do. Fortunately for you your arrival is actually quite fortuitous. You see I have to leave on business shortly earlier than I'd anticipated, so, Ferrari? Italian, yes?" Mr Leony then asked.

"Well, yeah, of course. Like the car. Quick and seductive. I am the rearing stallion. Ain't you ever seen *Magnum P.I.?* You know, the T.V. show?"

"I have not, no. Why, was he Italian?"

"Who Tom Selleck? No, I don't think so but the car definitely was. The car was the show. The same could've been said about *The Dukes of Hazzard* and Kitt the talking car who was basically the star of *Knight Rider.* Do you really think anyone gave a fuck about David Hasselhoff? No way!"

"What?" Mr Leony wondered, baffled by Lawrence's response.

"What I'm saying is that it was all about the car. Even when he moved to *Baywatch* still nobody gave a fuck about him. The reason that show was one of the biggest of all time? As if I need to tell you. Running dripped wet silicon enhanced babes in tight red lifeguard swim suits juggling their huge breasts! It couldn't fail. It's a born winner. Sex sells and everybody knows that. Why do you think they put hot chicks on the bonnets of cars? Cos it shifts more cars, simple. They trade off one and other perfectly. It's a partnership made in heaven as far as the car industry and dealers who sell them are concerned. The car sales market is geared toward catering for men because they buy the larger percentage of automobiles. Fact. Cars are also commonly referred to as 'she', she being the adjective to describe a female. So men obviously consciously or subconsciously think of their cars as women. Ergo there's plainly a lesbian love fantasy thing going on that men have created between cars and women. There's a very distinct correlation that links the two. Why they've never teamed up a sexy chick and an exotic sports car is beyond me. And if they have I ain't seen it," Lawrence rattled out, his nerves now clearly getting the better of him.

"Okay, okay. Stop please! Have you been drinking? Are you high? And is this going anywhere? Because you're giving me a fucking migraine over here. You know you don't sound much like any butler I've even known," Mr Leony said, sceptical of Lawrence and his strange mannerisms.

"Sorry, sir."

"Look, just being Italian and knowing about women, fast cars and how they relate to one another will not win my favour. I'm not some two-bit car dealer looking for tips on how to make up my monthly quota. And I sure as hell couldn't care less about your trivial knowledge of cheesy action programming during the bleak spell in history often referred to as the eighties. None of those things are any use to you here. Understand?!" Mr Leony barked, still trying to weigh Lawrence up.

"I thought the eighties rocked. Of course not, sorry. I talk too much. I'm just nervous. First day on the job, you know. And I do watch too much television. But then broadcasting's loss is your gain, my friend. And I actually coincidentally used to do a little work in the T.V. and movie business," Lawrence said, trying his best to impress Mr Leony.

Mr Leony stopped and turned around raising his index finger sharply into the air directly in front of Lawrence's face. "Shut and listen! I have no interest in that. You are not family and you are not

36

my friend, so don't presume to know me when you don't. Not too many men have made that mistake. And those who have. Well, use your fucking imagination. And I'll say this too. You sure as hell ain't true blood Italian. But if you work hard and show me loyalty then the rewards can be high. But know that I do not suffer fools gladly, and the job I have for you is of paramount importance. Muck this up and I'll personally torture you in numerous painful ways. But I would not kill you. Death would be too quick and easy. No, I'd keep you on the brink of survival so that you can be Randy's wild-play-sex-thing. A fate worse than death I can assure you," he warned.

"Ah, ah, ah! Funny. Please don't feel that you need to put me at ease. Just give it to me straight. Don't hold back or nothin'. I've heard about you rich playboy types, and I gotta say I ain't into any kinky shit. So it's a case of Randy by name, Randy by nature, eh?" Lawrence giggled, he should've got out there and then but as before he tried to blag his way around it.

"I wouldn't be so cool, Mr Ferrari. You seem to be under the mistaken impression that I'm joking. I assure you that I am not. I don't joke. He's my highly sexually charged orangutan. Yes, I thought that might wipe the smile from your face," Mr Leony said, as Lawrence's gormless grin turned south. "Believe me, it wiped the smile from mine. He has quite the formidable grip. I won him in a raffle would you believe." he then continued.

"A raffle?"

"Yes, a raffle. I'd never really won anything before that day. Well, not without death threats, blackmail or bribing somebody. So you can imagine my surprise when my number was called. But nothing could prepare me for the shock of what it was. That's the last time I hold a charity fund raising benefit dinner in aid of your starving cousins in Africa. Of that you can be sure. If they're so fucking hungry why don't they eat the fat sex crazed ape. It would've saved me a lot of time and money. I have to put him in a loincloth, you know, cos he's permanently aroused. All of the time! It's an embarrassment. My dear old mother doesn't know where to look. I would've shot and mounted the damn thing over the fireplace long ago, but my kids, they love him."

"Yeah, kids. But they're the future. Wait, loincloth? You sure you're not thinking of Tarzan? Sorry, no problem, Mr Leony," Lawrence said, now nervous as hell.

"Good, that's what I like to hear. No ifs, buts or maybes. And I suppose if Frankie from the agency sent you then you must be good, if a tad unorthodox perhaps. Alas, I don't have time to see for myself as I say."

"Ah yes, Frank. My mentor. More of a father figure actually. And I like to think of my methods as yes unorthodox, but also challenging and progressively evolving to break new ground in a bid not only to better myself but also to better the service that I ultimately provide."

"Father figure? Frankie? Frankie is a woman for Christ's sake!" bellowed Mr Leony.

"Yes, precisely. But not just any woman. A woman with real balls. A leader. A boss. And hence a man," Lawrence responded quickly, now completely working off the script.

After an initial uncomfortable silence that seemed to last an eternity, Mr Leony erupted into laughter. It was almost as if he'd just got the punchline to a joke. "HAHHH! AHHHH! You're right there. You know I think I'm gonna like you, Mario. You seem a stand-up guy. I'm beginning to see what Frankie sees in you. You're not short of balls yourself," Mr Leony then said as he slapped Lawrence enthusiastically across the back.

"Haaaa! Thank you, sir."

"Anyway, I will be gone for the weekend. My usual butler has taken ill shall we say. So you will have to take care of my mother. She loves television also. You'll both get on like a house on fire. See to it she's kept warm and comfortable, but for God's sake mind your language. I don't care, but she hates any cussing. If you have any problems whatsoever, phone me. My number's on the fridge along with some further instructions, her medication dosage and what not. Nothing to worry about. Right, see you in a couple of days. Consider this to be a trial period. Impress me and who knows. Maybe I won't kill you." Mr Leony chuckled as he turned and made his way towards his waiting limo.

That night Mrs Leony was particularly restless wanting something to eat or drink every few minutes. When she complained that she was too cold Lawrence saw to it and got a roaring fire going. But still she wouldn't shut up. Then there was that bell. Whenever she wanted something she'd ring the damn thing until he came running. It was enough to drive him up the wall. He couldn't take much more. It was utterly exhausting. He began to wonder if she'd driven the previous butler to the brink of total despair and eventual suicide.

RING! RING! RING! Mrs Leony chimed over and over again.

"Yes, Mrs Leony? What is it this time?" Lawrence muttered from behind clenched teeth.

"You're not Arthur, nigger! What have you done with him? I want Arthur! Go away. Get your dirty hands away from me!" Mrs Leony shrieked as she stabbed at Lawrence accusingly with her bony little finger.

Nothing was ever said about the old bat being completely senile. Not to mention a horrible racist. That seemed to be a minor detail Mr Leony conveniently 'forgot' to divulge.

"Not this again. I told you. He's not well. And we've met already. Remember? Your son hired me to look after you while he's away. He'll be home before you know it. So what do you want?"

"Murderer! What have you done with Arthur?" Mrs Leony screeched.

"Murderer?! What? Who said anything about murder? Look, lady, I don't know Arthur. But I'm sure he's fine."

"Liar!"

On Lawrence's six or seventh visit to the kitchen looking for her bottle of brandy he came across a box of dog tranquilliser pills. He figured he could use some of them on her and maybe she'd fall asleep for a while. After all, where was the harm in that? So he crushed a few up and added them to her drink. Lawrence then took both the glass and bottle through to her. She promptly snatched the glass and downed all its contents before stubbornly refusing to give the bottle of brandy back. Lawrence was way too tired and fed up to argue. She seemed content so he just left her to it. Lawrence instead went into the next room to start bagging up any items of value that he could find and was undisturbed for some time. Mrs Leony was out cold in the next room due to the simple fact that alcohol and sleeping tablets are twice as potent when working together. However, the bottle of brandy had fallen from her frail and weakened hands and smashed on the fireplace bursting into flames. Little did Lawrence know, but while he struggled to decide what to steal next, poor old Mrs Leony was being burned alive in the very next room. Lawrence only became aware of this when the paint on his side of the door began to bubble and blister. As smoke soon followed from under the door he realised too late what had happened. His worst fears were confirmed seconds later as he frantically checked Mr Leony's desk to switch on a security camera feed of the next room. All he could make out was Mrs Leony's jammed on electric wheelchair zipping left then right in and out of shot, now nothing more than a flaming ball of fire. With the piercing sound of fire alarms still screaming in his ears he leapt into his car to make good his escape, but in the rush and panic he crashed a few blocks down the street. Luckily he managed to disappear into the night before being found.

Chapter 4

The next morning brought heavy rain made worse by a cold wind which whistled at Morgan's window rattling the pane. To the inside of the glass an intricately fine and almost transparent layer of frost was beginning to melt over the heat from the radiator below causing condensation to drip down and gather in small puddles on the windowsill.

Morgan was still in bed enjoying the last of his own self-contained warmth beneath the covers. It seemed to have taken all night to reach this level of comfort, and soon he'd have to reluctantly get up and face the day. As he lay there exposed only from the neck up, he caught sight of something out of the corner of his eye. To begin with it appeared to be fairly miscellaneous, a wall tack or a small dark smudge perhaps. But no. It was alive. And moved. It definitely moved. It got nearer and was humungous. Surely this wasn't a normal sized spider Morgan thought. What he saw bore more resemblance to some kind of strange mutant hairy hand.

"Oh, just bloody marvellous." Morgan grimaced. But he wasn't giving up his spot. Not without a fight. As he lay there perfectly snug he followed the arachnid's intended route hoping it'd change direction or suddenly die of a heart attack. Anything but come towards him. It, however, just got closer and closer until Morgan could not bear the spider's presence any longer. So he leapt out from under his duvet and donned his dressing gown leaving the once warm, safe sanctuary of his bed. Spider one. Morgan nil. A formidable foe for sure.

Unsurprisingly Morgan was the first up. Stuart was still in what can only really be described as a coma that somehow he was able to break out of every now and then. Morgan made his way through the living room from his bedroom passing by the front door as he walked into the kitchen. He poured himself a large glass of Iron Brew to try and salivate his mouth once more as he sat on the edge of a kitchen stool. Sitting there he cast his eye over what he called home and was disgusted. He couldn't remember the last time he'd seen the carpet in the living room, let alone recall its colour. Even if he lifted all the rubbish from off the floor there was still an almost uncleanable layer of decaying food and nondescript matter below. Morgan couldn't stand it. He hated it to the point where he began a mission almost impossible, the noise of which must have startled Stuart who emerged at his bedroom door looking not unlike an uncooked pork sausage.

"Morgan, mate. Whatcha doin'?" Stuart yawned as he stood there rubbing his eyes.

"It's called cleaning and tidying up. Ever heard of the practice? Raymond is planning that inspection the day. Sae Ah'm shifting this revolting mess. Which Ah fear may be alive by the way. Ah mean Ah'm sure that Ah saw it move. We're probably breeding some kinda new strain ay flesh eating bacteria in here, man. And Ah think it's givin' me a rash in aw," Morgan explained, with a genuine look of concern etched across his face.

"It's nae that bad. It's like something we've grown and cultivated. Ah like tae think ay Barry as a pet," Stuart contested as he relit an old tabbed cigarette from off the floor from the night before.

Morgan looked up at Stuart from all fours, "Wait, 'Barry'? Ye've actually named this mess, Barry? Dae Ah look like Alan Titchmarsh tae ya? Dae ah? No, exactly! Ah'm nae proud ay the fact that we've given birth tae some kinda sub mutagenic livin' fungal carpet. Ah'm tellin' ya it'll turn on us like that film, *Little Shop Ay Horrors*."

"Now Ah think yer being a tad melodramatic. Ah said Ah would dae it and Ah will," Stuart said, now holding his stomach and looking slightly uneasy.

"Aye, sae ya did. But when? In ma lifetime?"

"Soon."

"Yer good at that, aren't ya? Good at sayin' ye'll dae something when in actual fact ye dae bugger aw!"

"Fine, fair play. Let's have some breakfast and then tackle this bad boy together. Many hands make stuff easier or whatever," Stuart replied, feeling ever more anxious and the look on his face ever more uncertain.

Morgan looked up at Stuart once again, "Aye, that would be nice but there's arse aw tae eat, sae let's cut the bollocks and bullshite

42

mantra and just get on wi it. Unless that is ya want tae empty aw the mouse pellets from the cutlery drawer intae a bowl, lob some milk on it and call it Coco Pops. It may very well turn the milk chocolate but it'll taste suspiciously like…" Morgan began as he tried to motivate Stuart into assisting him. Stuart, however, was now in a trance as he stared blankly at the floor which only served in frustrating Morgan even further. "Well, ya nob?" Morgan continued, but still there was no reply from Stuart who by then was hopping from one foot to the other like he was doing a wee an Irish jig or perhaps more accurately some kind of jobby dance.

"Ssstuuuarrrt?" Morgan whispered, now utterly exasperated.

Breaking out of his stupor Stuart edged tentatively toward the bathroom. "Please tell me we have bog roll," he then said with a nervous shudder.

"Okay. But Ah'd be lying." Morgan smiled as he informed Stuart now realising his plight and revelling in it.

At that Stuart tensed and reached sharply down to grab a handful of rubbish from off the floor by the front door before locking himself in the toilet. There followed some minutes of deathly silence, then without so much of a warning Stuart thundered back out of the toilet screaming, "YES! YES! YES! YA FUCKIN' DANCER! AH FUCKIN' KNEW IT! Dae ya know what this is?" and waving a very soggy brown piece of paper frantically in front of Morgan who was understandably quite unable to share in Stuart's uncontrollable celebration.

Morgan chanced a look. "Aye, Ah dae. It's a piece ay shite-stained paper. Nah, wait. It's our shite-stained mail. And there's absolutely nae need tae stick it down ma throat. Ah understand ye dinnae like bills, but then who does?"

Stuart held it close in front of Morgan. "Take a closer look. Ah think ye'll find it's worth millions."

The realisation knocked the wind out of Morgan like an awkward fall. "Oh, ma God! Is that really what Ah think it is?" he then gulped with a shocked gaze on his face before continuing. "Ah cannae believe ya wiped yer hole wi it, ya dirty bastard. That's gotta be the more expensive arse wipe in history. And it's covered in jobby!"

Stuart ran into the kitchen where he emptied the sink of dirty dishes before running the winning ticket gently under the tap. Once clean he slapped it on top of the radiator to dry. Morgan was still noticeably stunned and had gone for a short lie down on the sofa to try and process what this meant. He was soon joined by Stuart who was thinking the exact same thing. How to get to America? Okay, it wasn't Morgan's first thought but it came a very close second.

"Okay, it would seem yer not talkin' total pish after all. Which now begs the question. How dae we get tae America?" Morgan said.

"Weird, you were thinkin' that in aw?"

"Well, d'ah! Hmmm? Well, Ah guess if we both... together stole... in fact took back ma bike we could afford some cheap tickets," Morgan then proposed.

Stuart nodded in agreement. "Ah suppose it's worth a try. Although, that's a lot ay taxi rides. And we can only take one punter at a time in the sidecar. We'll be ferrying folk about for donkeys before we make enough cash."

"No, dummy. We sell the bike." Morgan sighed.

"Right. That was actually ma plan B. But we'll try that first."

"Sae we better tell Raymond we may be moving out. At least we willnae have tae worry about that inspection. Looks like we get the last laugh after aw," Morgan added, now smiling from ear to ear.

"Sweet," Stuart purred in full agreement.

On leaving the flat they were both plunged into darkness. 'It' had turned off the hall light in an ever expanding plan to save money, but within seconds the switch was found narrowly avoiding a potentially embarrassing limb breaking catastrophe. So they crept slowly down the stairs. Then when outside Raymond's flat Stuart knocked on the door. It however just creaked ominously open. The room was in semi-darkness as the curtains were still drawn from the night before. The only source of light came from the television and from around the edges of the curtains.

"Hello, Raymond? Are ya there?" Morgan whispered as he peered hesitantly into the room.

"Ya stinkin' fat twat," Stuart added.

"Shut it, you!" Morgan muttered as he wrenched Stuart back by the scruff of the neck.

There was no reply, but still Morgan was on his guard. He was a coiled spring expecting him to pop out of the shadows at any given moment. Stuart on the other hand just barged past Morgan and made his way into the room as bold as brass before sitting on the footrest section of Raymond's reclining chair in front of the telly.

"What in Christ's sake dae ya think yer daein'?" Morgan exclaimed as he crouched down on the floor in some kind of lame half-hearted attempt to conceal himself.

Stuart didn't even bother straining his neck to look around. His eyes were firmly fixed on the television. "He's obviously nipped out. And he's got a functioning telly. Sae Ah'm watching *Deal or No Deal*. Who woulda thought opening boxes could be sae exciting. There's no questions or nothing either. Brilliant," he then declared before cranking up the volume on the T.V. to such a level that next door's dog had started to howl. Yet he still hadn't noticed Raymond's dead body slumped on the chair behind him, mainly because the lighting in the room was only sufficient enough to pick up the silhouettes of certain objects close to him.

"Ah doubt it. And are ya fuck watchin' *Deal or No Deal*. Get outta there now. And turn it down anaw before Ah slap ya one. He wouldnae just leave the telly on and the door open. It's nae that kinda neighbourhood." Morgan cringed, convinced they were going to get caught red-handed.

"Are ya comin' in then or no? And maybe while yer at it check the kitchen tae see if ya can find some nachos or biscuits. Ma guts are hangin', man," Stuart asked as he turned around to face Morgan for the first time.

As he did so he caught a glimpse of the body in front of him but he wasn't altogether sure so he leaned forward. In doing so he exerted his entire weight onto the footrest.

"OH FUCKIN' HELL!" Stuart screamed out like a schoolgirl in fully-fledged panic as the chair folded back up forcing him hard to the floor. This also caused the back of the chair to spring violently forward into an upright position which in turn propelled Raymond towards Stuart in one swift catapulting action. There was nothing he could do. The weight on top of him was too great. He could barely breathe but still there followed a very faint and muffled cry for help from beneath Raymond's corpse.

"Stuart, what the hell are ya daein' now? He could arrive any minute. Yer makin' far tae much noise," Morgan whispered, oblivious to Stuart's dilemma.

Stuart managed to squeeze his head from under Raymond's shoulder. "He's already here, ye arsehole," he then spat out as he attempted to body press Raymond to one side but instead remained firmly pinned to the floor.

Morgan assumed Stuart had seen him outside and was hiding behind the chair. So he sniped across the carpet to join him.

"Where? And wow, did ya fart? Cos that's rotten, dude, even by yer vile standards."

"Right here for fuck's sake!" Stuart groaned as he started to lose consciousness.

"Where?" Morgan asked, his eyes searching the room.

Stuart was running out of time. "Help! Turn on the light... quickly!" he then pleaded.

Morgan hesitated but did eventually reach around to switch on a table lamp which lit up Stuart's nightmarish predicament. When Morgan turned around to see what the problem was the shock knocked him back into a line of shelves which clattered down to the floor by his feet.

"Hold on!" Morgan panted as he pulled himself up and began to tug Raymond off Stuart who by then had almost choked to death himself. Stuart however managed to roll free but was left gasping for breath.

"Ah think they're broken," Stuart sobbed as he nursed his ribs.

"Are ya okay, fella?" Morgan asked, helping Stuart to his feet.

"Fuck-fuckidy-fuck-fucker! No, Ah'm far from fuckin' okay! And as for you ya fuckin' fat pile ay fuck! What's the craic, man? Fuck!" Stuart yelled as he proceeded to talk down to Raymond's lifeless body.

"Wow! Calm the jets."

"God fuckin' damn it! Jump at me will ya? Dinnae just lie there! Answer me, ya bawbag!" Stuart continued as he began to kick at Raymond's ample frame.

46

"Stop it!" Morgan cried, but again his plea fell on deaf ears.

"Ah cannae believe ya did that. What in sweet fuck dae ya think yer daein'? Ye scared the livin' shite outta me! What's yer game?" Stuart bellowed, kicking him again and again.

"Stop! Stop kickin' him!" Morgan shouted as he stooped down to examine Raymond.

"Wha?"

"Dae ya no see he's... he's deid!"

"What do ya mean, deid? As in deid, deid?"

"As opposed tae deid alive."

"How dae ya know? Yer no doctor."

"The lack ay physical or vocal reaction tae ya kickin' him in the stomach perhaps. He's stone cold. And finally, and this clinched it by the way, the absence ay a pulse. Look, he's as white as a sheet. In fact, he's blue. Sae ya see, Ah dinnae huvtae be a doctor. Unless ya think that's normal," Morgan asked, pointing to the deceased body before them.

"Well, Ah didnae kill im'. Did Ah?"

"Nobody's sayin' ya did, Stuart. Ah think he was a stiff well before we got here. Look, lift his arm and it stays there. His face is like playdough. Ya can change his expression and it stays like that. Rigor mortis is definitely present here."

"Well, what did he die ay? And close his eyes. That shit is freakin' me out. It's like he's watchin' us. His eyes are following me like some kinda freaky painting. And please stop playin' wi im', man. He's deid, no an action figure."

"He died ay. Ah dunno? Maybe he died ay fat-smelly-bastard-itus."

"This is bad. Sae really we should leave. Right now," Stuart decided, already halfway out the door.

"We cannae leave. He's dead. Shouldn't we inform someone?" Morgan said, drawing the curtains across fully.

"NO! No, because... because Ah'm involved in a highly sensitive F.B.I witness protection and relocation programme and that. Naebody must even know Ah even exist. Ah was wearing a wire, man. A fuckin' wire! Huv ya any idea what they'll dae tae me?

Ah hoped that ye wouldnae find out this way. Ah've put aw our lives in jeopardy. Ah'm sorry. They're probably watchin' us right now!"

"Really? That's yer best excuse?"

"Okay, okay. Ah ate a bucketload ay those prawns earlier. Ah just cannae stay here any longer. It's turning my stomach. Ah've already nearly shat masel this mornin'. Ah'm kinda turtle heidin' it right now tae be honest. Ah really dinnae feel right," Stuart confessed.

"Prawns? Oh, aye. Like the ones… no the ones from the back ay the fridge in the cardboard container marked 'South Sea takeaway'? Tell me for God's sake it wasnae them." Morgan checked knowing very well that they were way past their best. In fact, they were probably past their best at the time.

"Aye, that's right. That place is still open? Ah thought it closed down last month. Anyway, they're starting tae repeat on me. And wi the smell and the body, no tae mention him lying on me, Ah feel a wee bit fragile and that. Why dae ya ask?"

"Oh, no reason. Ya feel fine though, right? Ah mean other than dodgy guts."

"Ah guess."

"Okay then. We can thank our lucky stars that ya huv the metabolism ay a mountain goat. Now, coming back tae the issue in hand, i.e. the body. And believe me it's nae ma idea ay fun either, but we cannae leave him like this. Especially wi his arm up in the air the way it is. It'd probably be best if Ah put it back down. Ah keep thinking he wants tae pitch in wi a solution on how tae remedy our problem." Morgan smirked.

"This is no funny, man. And are ya sure that we cannae leave 'im? Ah mean yer right. We cannae just leave 'im. No, ay course no. That'd be wrong and highly irresponsible… Unless, maybe we could. Hear me out. He never gets visitors. Why would he? He's a monumental twat. That's well established. And Ah figure that we'll be in the States a week, a week and a half max. Then we're back. Sae maybe he could wait here until then. Hey, it's just a thought. Ah personally think it could grow legs. What say ye?"

"That's yer plan? Really? If ya think ya can jam him in the freezer perhaps. Huv ya the slightest idea what his body is goin' tae look like after a week and a half? We're talkin' rottin' human flesh here. We're talkin' pupatin' fly larvae. That means maggots, man. Millions ay squirmin' burrowin' wormy-like carnivores wrigglin' around in his eye sockets. And a smell sae foul yer skid marked Y-fronts would pale in comparison. Stuart, are ya cool? Ah mean, ye look weird. Like ill. Yer green. Yer actually green. Normally it's a figure of speech or sommit ya see in cartoons. But no for real. No really. But yer literally green. Yer no goin' tae pass out are ya?"

"Nah, Ah'm cool. Ah'm feelin' brand new by the way. Fuckin' solid me. Ah'm in complete control. HHHOOOOAAAAH!" Stuart assured Morgan before promptly going on to vomit everywhere.

"Ah count six, no seven chunks ay carrot. What about you? What's up wi that anyway? There's always carrot. Even if ya never touch the stuff. And you never eat vegetables anyway. Yer the polar opposite ay a vegetarian. Oh, hello. What's that? An undigested prawn heid. Eeewwhooo!" Morgan said, diving out of the way before being plastered by a steady stream of projectile vomit.

"Hhheeeaaawwwiii.i.i.i!" Stuart continued, bent over double and shuddering like an epileptic at a disco.

"That truly is one ay the most disgusting things that Ah huv ever witnessed. And in two long years livin' wi you that's really sayin' sommit. First the diarrhoea. Now the pukin'. Somebody cork this boy. At both ends. Tell ya what, Ah'll run back upstairs faster than a cheetah on heat and throw some stuff in a bag and think about what the hell we're goin' tae dae. You, you wait here and finish barfin'," Morgan said as he made his way back to their flat.

Morgan was gone just long enough for Stuart to stumble across an old tin that must've fallen down along with the shelves. On looking inside Stuart found that it was in fact jammed full of money. Probably their rent from over the years.

"That's a pretty small bag, Morgan. A Tesco carrier bag tae be exact. Huv ya packed enough stuff? Looks like the P.E. days back at school. Ah trust there's more than just a T-shirt, shorts, tin ay Lynx and a pair ay smelly old runners in there?"

"Sure, Ah reckon we travel light. Aw we really need are spare under crackers, our passports and the winnin' lotto ticket. Ah figure that we can just buy new clothes or whatever else over there. How about you though? Feel better?"

"Aye, and maybe finding aw this money has sommit tae dae wi it." Stuart revealed, holding up the tin of cash.

"What money?"

"Err? Nae money. Who said anything about money?" Stuart said, back peddling fuelled by Morgan's reaction.

"Stuart."

"No, fuck it! Our money. Our goddamned money. Look, he's been hoarding it. He's tighter than tae coats ay paint, man. We need this money," urged Stuart.

"It's his tae hoard. Ah ain't stealin' from no dead dude. That shit ain't right. Ah've already decided tae leave Ray here and turn a blind eye against ma better judgement."

"Really?"

"There's nothin' tae implicate us in this. And nae amount ay medical intervention can save him now. Sae we'll just carry on as if we never found im' and somebody else will. We'll maybe make an anonymous phone call or sommit. If we hang around here we'll never get away. After all, time's money. Quite literally."

"Thank God. And we need this money anaw. There's nae way Ah'm leavin' it here wi that magpie bastard. Now he's croaked it, it's ours. Finders keepers. Ah tell ya what ye should be worryin' about. Those devil dogs. How are ya planning tae get rid ay them. That bike is our transport and they stand between us and it," Stuart said, cunningly changing the subject away from his newly pilfered money.

"Feed 'em yer puke. Ah dunno? Those evil bastards cost me five quid let's no forget. Ah tell ya, it's the least they deserve," Morgan said, but wasn't really being serious.

"Ya know it's sae low, repugnantly vile, totally cruel and basically goes against everythin' that Ah believe as an active member ay Greenpeace. But in the name ay curiosity and science Ah say we try it. We're almost obligated. It might just work. It is after aw a kinda recycling. If it doesnae work, we'll just huvtae use you as some sort ay lure."

Morgan laughed. "None ay that is true. And no way. That's a terrible plan."

"Is it, Morgan? If ya ask me it's a damn fine plan. It looks pretty solid stuff. We could spoon it up. Ah mean a lot ay dogs will happily eat their own shite. Ah've seen em' dae it. Maybe they'll dig this, a new culinary sensation for them."

"Yer one sick guy. No pun intended. Ye need help. Seriously, dude."

"Boom, boom," Stuart drummed.

Stuart made for Raymond's kitchen where he rummaged around looking for a suitable tool for the job. After making a rather large mess he eventually found a Tupperware container and a ladle. When he returned he scooped some of it up and they made their way down the road to Fat Tam's scrapyard. When they arrived Morgan gave the fence a good rattle and sure enough they came running out. So Stuart pulled the lid off the container and forced it under the fence. However, they just circled the box giving it the odd semi-curious sniff.

"Ah told ya. They're nae gonna touch that filth. Why would they? They're nae that daft. A big juicy steak or sommit like that woulda been the one," Morgan said shaking his head.

Morgan had no sooner said it when one of the dogs started to lap it up. Next thing you know they actually started to fight over it. Now they had the diversion they so sorely needed.

"Nonsense. Ye wanted revenge. Givin' em' a decent meal isnae revenge. That's right, tuck in while it's still fresh and warm, ya fuckers," Stuart said, quietly coaxing them.

Morgan pushed Stuart forward, "On ya go then. Shit before the shovel."

The dogs seemed to have lost all interest in them so they started to open the gate, slowly at first, but as the level of vomit began to steadily drop they moved with more urgency. Once the gate was fully opened they crept passed the dogs and made their way directly to the bike which was only a matter of metres away.

"Where are the dogs?" Morgan gasped, aware he'd lost sight of them.

"Who cares? Just get on the bike!"

The bike spluttered and jolted into life first time so Stuart leapt into the sidecar. The dogs on the other hand were lying in the middle

51

of the road whining and flinching violently. It would seem, unsurprisingly, that regurgitated off prawns didn't much agree with them either. Morgan only just managed to swerve to avoid them as he sped past.

"Morgan, you coulda killed 'em!" Stuart cried over the noise of the engine.

"Are you forgetting that it was yer stomach contents they ate?" Morgan replied.

"Touche!"

"Stuart, are you sure ya huv the ticket?"

"Cha-ching!" Stuart said waving it in the air.

"Tae the airport then!"

Chapter 5

One of life's biggest nightmares must be watching your home burn to the ground. Everything you have accumulated and worked for, all of those irreplaceable memories, gone in a matter of hours. How would you then feel if your own mother was burned alive in that very same fire? Then, to top it all off you found out it was no accident and you knew exactly who was responsible. Pissed off is how you'd feel. And that's putting it mildly. Anger would drive you to revenge. Most of us would want the same for the person that caused it. An eye for an eye. At the very least you'd want them to rot in prison forever.

Mrs Leony was nothing but an unrecognisable smouldering pile of ashes among the rest of burned debris from the Leony mansion. He knew precisely who had killed his mother and he wanted nothing more than to blow Lawrence Lowmax's brains out. Lawrence, however, was nowhere to be found, but that didn't mean he was safe. Far from it. He now had a heavy price on his head. So if a bounty hunter didn't get him one of Mr Leony's paid assassins undoubtedly would. The irony being that prison, at least for now, was probably the safest place for Lawrence to be. He was in effect off the grid. The last place Rico Leony would think of looking was the state penitentiary.

After being run over Lawrence had been understandably quite badly injured but recovered a few months into his sentence. Nevertheless, he decided not to let on about his improvements, mainly because he'd come to realise being in a weakened and vulnerable position brought him sympathy with both prison wardens and inmates alike. This meant he got more privileges which included extra day releases. It was also around this time that he first received a letter from a family links agency telling him about a nephew in Britain. To begin with he paid it no attention, but he knew with continued good behaviour he may get out sooner than expected. He decided to answer it, the idea being that if he had a contact in another country he may be able to flee America. At least until the heat died down. He kept in touch with Stuart and even used his suggested numbers in a lottery ticket that he purchased on a release day. Never for one second did he believe it'd actually win. Things really got complicated when it did. Just picture it, this helpless guy in a rowdy prison watching his numbers roll out one by one and knowing he'd won. He wanted nothing more than to collect his winnings and bank it. Unfortunately, he'd used up all of his prison breaks so there was no way of getting the money himself. He certainly wasn't going to tell anybody in prison, so his only chance of getting his hands on it lay in yet another gamble – Stuart. Now as far as Lawrence was concerned Stuart wasn't related to him, and even if somehow he was he didn't care. It had all been some kind of administration or computing error, but as long as Stuart was convinced the money was safe. So the lotto ticket was sent to Stuart in the hope he'd collect the millions and pay Lawrence's bail to get him out. Lawrence now had a chance, albeit a small one, assuming that he could stay off the radar and remain hidden from Mr Leony and his hired guns.

Rico Leony had moved to his beach house out of the city to avoid the press and T.V. news frenzy that ensued following Mrs Leony's abrupt departure from this world. He'd contacted some of his very best men to meet up to discuss his plans.

Steve Hickman, Karl Sharp and Marcus Dyson were the men Mr Leony had called upon and hoped would resolve his problem.

"I WANT HIS SEVERED HEAD ON A FUCKING POLE! Do you understand me? I want him to know what it's like to try and pick up his own teeth with broken fingers!" Mr Leony bellowed, barely able to contain his fury.

"Calm down," Marcus began. "It will be done, Rico. Don't worry. At least we know who this jerk-off really is. Karl, fill the man in." he then continued in an attempt to cool Rico's mood.

"Yeah, I did a little digging. I got an old associate to do a background check. His name ain't Mario Ferrari for a start," explained Karl.

"Fucking knew he wasn't Italian," Rico fumed.

"Right, he's Lawrence Lowmax. He works in the fucking movie business if you can believe that. Or at least he used to. As a make-up artist or some shit. He did some low budget horror and sci-fi flicks but he got into some kinda altercation with a director on set. They kicked him out and he hasn't been welcome back. Since then he's been picked up on a couple of misdemeanours and has been involved in some pretty low level stuff. He's now a suspected con man. I have the file here and it makes for quite an interesting read," Karl added as he tossed the dossier onto Rico's desk.

Rico took one look at it and then threw it flying to one side. "I DON'T CARE ABOUT THIS SHIT! I just want that fuck screaming in pain! I ain't looking for some light bedtime reading!"

"Rico, please. We need level heads on this. You're not thinking straight. I don't want to appear flippant or to trivialise your loss, that's the last thing I'd wanna do and I hope you know that, but please calm down. Besides, you ain't much good to anyone if you drop dead from a heart attack now, are you?" Marcus begged, again appealing to Rico to take a step back.

Mr Leony's hand shook as he poured himself another large whisky. The adrenaline coursing through his veins caused his entire body to tremble. "Calm down? You're telling me to calm down? That lowlife degenerate fuck killed my mother! I want to skin and boil him alive in salty water, then watch him drown in a sea of his own blood. You cannot, will not, let him escape! And with each minute that passes is a minute lost," Rico then continued with torture firmly in mind.

"Kinda like boil in the bag," muttered Steve.

"Shut up, Steve, you fucking asshole," Karl whispered forcefully as he lit up a cigarette.

Marcus could see the hurt burning in Rico's eyes. "I can only imagine what you must be feeling and anything I say will be of little consolation. But I am truly sorry, Rico. We go back a long way and I've never seen you like this before."

"That's cos my dear frail old mom ain't ever been murdered before! The only thing that I have left from the carnage that motherfucker single handily created is goddamned horny monkey! That's the only fucking thing that survived. Can you believe that?" Rico pointed out angrily, now fighting hard to hold the tears at bay and keep his composure.

"You have a monkey? Cool. What's his name?" Steve added, seemingly oblivious to the mood in the room.

"Steve. Please, for crying out loud," Karl groaned.

"Understand this, Rico. We never fail to get our man. He will pay for what he's done. Of that you can be sure. Just leave it to us. You should mourn your loss. Take some time out," Marcus assured Rico.

"I'll mourn when he's fucking dead!" Rico insisted.

Karl pulled hard on his cigarette as he looked over a photo of Lawrence. "Oh, trust me, this Lowmax character is already dead. He just doesn't know it yet." he then proceeded to push the glowing tip of his cigarette through the picture of Lawrence's head.

"So what movies did you say this joker has done?" Steve asked, totally unfazed by the emotional volatility of what was going on.

"Jesus Christ, Steve, I dunno?! I didn't get hold of his fucking portfolio," Karl hissed, realising that Steve was the potential match in a powder keg situation.

"I like movies. I was just curious to see if I might've seen anything he did is all," Steve sulked, confused by Karl's reaction.

"Anyway, you do realise that we could bring him to you. It's not our usual protocol, but given the circumstances I think an exception can be made. When we zero in and locate him we'll soften him up a little, naturally. It's kinda hard to avoid. Then knock his ass the fuck out and dump him in the trunk of Steve's car. After that it's just a simple case of driving him back here to hand deliver him to you. All wrapped up in a fucking bow if you want. That way you can get up close and personal. Have a little fun. You know you could really go to town on this guy. I fucking well would," Marcus suggested, quickly getting the subject of conversation back on course.

"Yeah, awesome. We call it the deluxe package," said Steve enthusiastically.

"What? No we don't." Marcus sighed.

"You talk about this as if I were booking a goddamned vacation to the Bahamas or something!" Rico exclaimed.

"Mr Rico, sir. You have absolutely nothing to worry about whatsoever. Like I mentioned earlier, I'm a bit of a movie buff. Ergo, I've seen a lot of movies. I've been thinking about all this long and hard. I know exactly what to do here," Steve continued.

"Movies?"

"That's right, movies. Just like this."

"Just like this?"

"Okay, not just like this, but the principle is the same. Kinda."

"I gotta say I'm not exactly getting filled with overwhelming confidence here, fellas," Rico questioned, now teetering on the edge as he looked in the direction of both Karl and Marcus for some kind of assurance.

"Steve, go get some fresh air," Karl ordered, pointing towards the door.

"I'm okay thanks."

"Go wait in the fucking car. Now!"

"What the fuck? Fine!" Steve grumbled as he made his way out of the room.

"Who the fuck was that guy?" Rico asked as the door slammed behind Steve.

"That's Steve. He's kinda new. Sorry, we didn't do any formal introductions. We were just so keen to press on given the situation. Look, the kid's as dumb as a post but he's one hell of a driver. He's gotten us outta more than just one tight spot. Right, Karl?" Marcus said, trying his best at a little damage limitation.

"Right, the kid's good. If a tad wet behind the ears. He's John's little brother. Remember John?" Karl then asked.

"Do I remember John? Of course. Wait, you're telling me that's John's little brother? Fuck me. You sure the apple fell from the same tree? Or even the same fucking orchard? And he's working with you guys now? Times really are hard," Rico mused.

"Yeah. Anyway, you're right, Rico. It's a ridiculous idea. Sorry, Marcus, but it is. I appreciate that you mean well but it's far too risky. We'll just cap him all nice and quiet like and send you a couple of snaps as souvenirs. Just like we usually do. No sense getting all creative now. Rico, you have too much to lose if this was to go sideways," warned Karl.

"No, I wouldn't say that at all. I may consider it as a very distinct possibility. I mean, let's face facts, people. This ain't usual. It's not your usual situation in that it doesn't usually happen!" Mr Leony disagreed.

"Okay then. The option is yours. We'll be in contact regardless," Marcus added.

"Gentlemen, nobody beyond these four walls and that dipshit outside should know about this. If the press were to get a hold of what is going on they'd have a field day. So as far as anybody else is concerned it was an accident. Aside from that particularly unpleasant and unfortunate happening it's business as usual," Rico stressed.

Marcus stood up. "Well, if that concludes our meeting I think we should get started."

Rico escorted them to the door. "Good hunting, gentlemen."

Chapter 6

Morgan and Stuart arrived at Glasgow airport cold and wet but nonetheless determined that they would make it to the States.

Morgan pulled up and stopped beside a car rental garage. "We're here! And sae far sae good, Stu boy." he then smiled broadly.

"Thank fuck for that! Ye drive sae slow. It's torture. We were overtaken by an old biddy on a mobility scooter at one point. It's embarrassing, dude. And it's nae exactly very comfortable in here either. Ma arse is about tae fall off here," Stuart moaned.

"What a gaylord. Yer the one complaining like an OAP."

"Anyway, where the hell are we gonna sell this bike?"

Morgan removed his helmet and killed the engine. "Ah'm going inside tae check out some flights. Yer going tae try and sell this bike over there. Can you handle that?" he then said, pointing confidently in the direction of a Hertz car rental garage.

"Piece ay piss, mate. Ah could sell snow tae the Eskimos. Stand aside."

"Great. Be ma guest. Just dinnae cock it up."

As Morgan made his way to the flights information desk in the main terminal, Stuart entered the car hire building to ask the manager if he'd be interested in purchasing their bike.

"Sorry, son. Ah dunno much about bikes? Cars are ma game. Plus, it's nae exactly company policy tae trade in private sales ay this nature," the managed explained.

"Are ya sure, pal? Ah'm in ay bit ay a jam here. Ah made a promise tae a friend sae Ah'm pretty desperate. We're talking knock-down bargain price here. Ah'm practically givin' it away," Stuart persisted.

"May Ah ask why?"

"Err? Ma mate Morgan was, err? Born with both lady and boy parts, sae we were kinda hoping tae travel tae America. Cos there's a top surgeon over there who specialises in gender reassignment. It's quite a sensitive subject if truth be told. Ah'm just going for moral

59

support," Stuart said lying through his teeth. He'd pretty much just gone with the first load of crap that popped into his head.

"Jesus! Really? That's awful. Well, Ah'd never normally dae this but tell ya what. Ah'll ask our mechanic, Ned. He might want tae take a look."

"Ah doubt Morgan would be up for that. Like Ah say he's super sensitive about it."

"No! Good God, man. The bike."

"Right."

"He's a bit ay a motorcycle enthusiast as a matter ay fact. If anybody's gonna take it off yer hands, then it'll be him," the manager said as he showed Stuart through the back to the garage workshop.

"Eh, Ned? Hi. Yer boss said it'd be cool tae huv a quick wee word wi ya," Stuart said introducing himself.

"Yeah. How can Ah help ye? Ah'm a little busy here right now," Ned muttered as he pulled himself out from under one of the cars he was working on.

"Dinnae ye worry. Ah willnae take up tae much ay yer time, chief. Basically, Ah was just wonderin' if ye'd be interested in buying a bike off me? Ah'm lookin' for a quick sale. Ya couldnae dae me a tremendous favour could ye?"

Once outside Ned looked over the bike and liked what he saw. "Aye, she's a beauty aw right. A classic. Sure she's seen better days, but with a bit ay restoration who knows. Ah could probably get her back tae her former glory days."

"Sae what are ye sayin'? Huv we a deal?"

"Look, Ah admire yer tenacity, but spit and polish aside Ah cannae afford her at the moment. No tae mention the time it'd take tae give her the TLC she deserves."

"Well, what can ye afford?" Stuart asked, undeterred by Ned's uncertainty.

"Very little. And it's even less now ma wife's left me. We were aw set tae jet off tae see *The Rolling Stones* in concert only a few days ago. A once in ay lifetime dream holiday doon the shitter! Ah'm no even daein' that now. Ah cannae bring masel tae. Wouldn't be the same without her. Bitch!"

60

"*The Stones*? Really? Sweet! It's a deal. Oh, and eh? Sorry about yer bird an that. What happened if ye dinnae mind me askin'?" Stuart beamed before feeling compelled to enquire on the circumstances of Ned's break up.

"Err? She left me for another woman if ye must know. No that it's any ay yer business," Ned said, taken aback by Stuart's forthrightness.

"Another woman? That's hot. Lesbians are awesome. Ah mean bummer, dude. Sorry," Stuart said before half-heartedly going on to try and console him.

"Sae anyway. Are yer sayin' ye'll swap this bike for ma tickets?"

"Too right, aye," Stuart said tossing him the keys.

"Ye've got yersel a deal."

Morgan meanwhile was having difficulty getting a flight of any description to America.

"I'm sorry, sir. We're fully booked up on that one too," said the woman at the check-in desk.

"There has tae be sommit, surely?" Morgan wasn't taking no for an answer.

"Not to California, no. I can't even get you a connecting flight. Not today anyway. I've a flight tomorrow morning at nine?"

"Hey, Morgan. How ya gettin' on?" Stuart asked as he strolled up behind him.

"Not well. There's nothin' until tomorrow at the earliest. Sae we either head back tae the flat and come back later or just hold up here and wait. How did ya get on sellin' the bike? How much did ya get? Please tell me good news."

"Not how much. Two tickets tae see *The Rolling Stones*! No bad, eh?" Stuart revealed excitedly.

"*The Stones*? *The Rolling Stones*? For fuck's sake, Stuart! Ah love *The Stones* as much as the next guy but Ah fail tae see how Mick, Keith and company are gonna help us outta this particular pickle. Ye really are a total bell-end! How the flyin' fuck can we afford two airfares now? Yer about as much use as ay wet fart in a spacesuit," Morgan said as he slapped the palm of his hand on his forehead.

61

"Chill, amigo. It's sorted. The Gods ay rock are smiling down on us," Stuart boasted as he handed over the tickets and began to strut about like Jagger.

"Sorted how exactly?"

"That's fine, sir. Any luggage?" the woman then asked, much to Morgan's amazement.

"Eh? No, just carry on. And him," Stuart said holding up their Tesco carrier bag and pointing at Morgan.

"Then your flight leaves in an hour and a half at gate eleven. If you'll just have your boarding passes and passports ready you can go straight through to the departure lounge. Have a nice trip, gentlemen," she continued, smiling at Stuart and then giving Morgan a quizzical look as if to say, "What the hell was that about?"

"How?" Morgan asked, still utterly baffled.

"Let's go take a seat and Ah'll explain," Stuart said, smugly.

The departure lounge was overflowing with people but there was still about five or six empty seats left next to a strange looking man dressed entirely in black. Morgan's immediate thought was one of curiosity and confusion. Why would some people be left standing in a busy terminal when there were clearly free seats available? Was he some kind of weirdo? Did he have extremely bad personal hygiene issues? Or was he just plain annoying?

"Sae what happened back there?" Morgan asked, still completely in the dark as to how Stuart had done what he'd done.

Stuart tucked their bag under his seat. "Ah swapped the bike for them just like ye asked. Ah told ya. Ah'm no totally useless."

"Aye, sae it would appear, but..."

"The tickets are tae see *The Stones* in concert. In California. They're daein' a tour ay the States as we speak. We huv flights and hotel aw included. Admittedly Ah didnae realise that at the time, but destiny is callin', ma friend. It's meant tae be. 'If you build it. They will come.' *Field Ay Dreams*. Ah loved that movie," Stuart said as he showed Morgan the tickets.

"Remarkable. We must be on some sorta lucky streak. Ah take it aw back, Stuart. Ye huv yer moments. Ah still dinnae fully understand what kinda Jedi mind trick ye used, but well done."

"Yeah. Ah'm pretty awesome."

"Alright. Dinnae push it. We know what yer like when ya get a big heid and start showing off. Being humble isn't yer strong point."

"Hey, Ah'm the world's best at being humble. Nobody even comes close."

"Ha, ha, okay then! Right yer are. Just dinnae jinx us now."

"Oh aye, while we're on the subject, there's a small catch. No big deal really."

"What?"

"Ye might have tae undergo gender reassignment," Stuart revealed.

"Excuse me?"

"Nothin'. Personal joke. Ye had tae be there." Stuart chuckled as he got up and made his way over to a television which was mounted about head height on the wall.

Morgan didn't move. He just sat there resting his eyes and tried to block out the noise around him, when he became aware of a low gravelly murmur, almost like a chanting sound. He opened his eyes and looked to his left without moving his head and saw that the strange man in black was saying something. What followed can only be described as strangely poetic:

I'm beginning to believe that I might very well be losing the plot.

My mask of sanity has slipped away and is nothing but a distant dot.

The strange voices and whispers in my head are all I've got.

Normality and who I was is something that I've left behind or forgot.

Cos I'm trapped in an odd place all alone in the freezing cold.

Everything is decomposing around me and I can see the mould.

I'm staring in the mirror but the person staring back looks twice as old.

I don't think the hand I once held is as strong so I'm going to have to fold.

Morgan swivelled away just as the man's head spun around to face him. Even though Morgan had turned and looked the other way, he could still feel the man's eyes boring into the back of his skull.

63

Morgan tried his best to ignore this uncomfortable feeling but it was obvious he'd seen him. Now he knew why the weirdo sat all alone.

"That was… interestin'. Kinda depressin' though if Ah'm completely honest. Ye know, dark. Got anythin' more upbeat?" Morgan said, hoping that he was just a pained poet and not a very good one at that.

"I know things. Secret things. They told me everything but they made me promise not to say. You can see them, can't you?" the stranger then asked quietly, before peering over his shoulder as if to make sure there was nobody else there.

"Who told ye what? And who Ah'm Ah meant tae be seein'?"

"The goblins," he then cackled maniacally.

"Goblins?"

"Yes, exactly. So you can see them too? They're everywhere. They control it all. We must stop them," the man whispered then giggled.

"Rrrright. Okay then. Unexpected, a little unnerving and scary. Yes, definitely scary… Err? Yes, anyway. Ah just remembered that Ah huv tae be… over there. Bye, bye now," Morgan said warily as he grabbed the bag from under his seat and bolted over to join Stuart.

The stranger however just sat there snickering and muttering to himself before seemingly falling unconscious.

"What are ye watchin'?" Morgan asked as he quickly double checked back over his shoulder to the comatose screwball he'd just escaped from.

"The news. Sae boring. Ah cannae seem tae get another chan…" Stuart began, but didn't get a chance to finish as a tannoy announcement came over the air.

"*BA flight 1475 to California now boarding at gate eleven,*" said an almost incoherent voice over the tannoy system.

"Was that us? Ah think it was. Why are those things sae hard tae understand in this day and age? Ah mean we managed tae sent a man tae the moon for Christ sake. And yet that sounded more like a kid underwater on an old walkie-talkie. Anyway, Ah suppose we should get movin'. Better take out the passports," Morgan then said, now raring to go.

In the noise and commotion of people frantically herding toward the plane nobody saw or heard the special news bulletin which flashed up on the television.

The news report read, *"...forcing the President to clamp down on the new splinter terrorist faction calling themselves the Jihadi Freedom Fighters. In other news, a Mr Raymond Lucus was found dead earlier today in what has been described as highly unusual and suspicious circumstances. Our sources say that police believe that the fifty-eight year old man may have been the victim of a vicious and systematic attack. So detectives are, for the time being, treating this case as a potential homicide. This won't be confirmed until further investigation and a report from the coroner's office is obtained. However, rumours persist that the victim had visible swollen marks around his neck suggesting foul play. His home also appears to have been ransacked. There are no eye witnesses as yet but the police are appealing to the general public for any useful information that may help further them in their enquiries. They would also very much like to get in contact with the two gentlemen from the flat above. So if this is you, or you recognise these men, then please get in touch. The number is at the bottom of your screens now. We'll keep you updated on that story as reports come in. Until then, here's 'Sunny Sue' with the weather. I'm Bob Sanders. Sky News."*

Chapter 7

The police were at Raymond's flat attempting to piece together what had happened. Detective Williamson and Detective Parker had been charged with heading the investigation. Both men had studied the scene for some time before coming to their quite separate conclusions.

"It seems tae me that the two…" Williamson began.

Parker looked at his notepad and flicked a few pages in. "Stuart Majors and Morgan Townsend."

"Aye, are our only real suspects," Williamson added.

"Suspects? Ah didnae realise we were even sure this was murder."

"Ye heard forensics. We've got a body wi what appears tae have strangulation marks. That doesnae strike ye as odd?"

"And the motives, sir?" Parker queried.

Williamson shook his head in disgust. "There's only one motive here, Parker. Personal gain. Ah mean look at the state ay this place. Somebody was lookin' for something, and Ah'd bet ma pension that's what's behind this."

"Sae what dae ye think they were after?"

"Probably money or sommit ay value. The usual. Maybe the rent. Who knows, they may huv simply got tired ay paying out aw that money month in, month out, sae hatched a diabolical plan tae take it back. Only Mr Lucus here didnae play ball. And there was ay altercation which ultimately resulted in murder," Williamson suggested.

Parker wasn't so sure. "Could it no simply be that perhaps the two gentlemen in the upstairs flat just stumbled across the body, panicked and fled the scene? One ay the two being physically sick which would explain the vomit. That's assuming they were even here in the first place. Ah mean tae be fair nothing appears tae be stolen. In fact, there doesnae seem tae be much ay value worth stealing. This is aw speculation at this juncture in time, surely?"

"Ah'm surprised at yer willingness tae overlook the obvious. There's nae mystery here as far as Ah'm concerned," Williamson concluded.

"That's no what Ah'm daein' at aw. If anything Ah'm just playin' devil's advocate here. We gotta keep our options open tae aw possibilities. It's just tae early tae say in ma humble opinion."

"Sae what direction dae ye think this investigation should take then? Ah mean, we gotta start somewhere."

"Agreed. There's just a few things that need explaining first."

"Like?" asked Williamson pointedly.

"Like the lack ay forced entry. Then there's the sick marks Ah mentioned before."

Williamson looked down to the vomit stains on the carpet. "Ah had wondered about the sick masel. But it looks like somebody has attempted tae clear it up. Seems unlikely that'd be Mr Lucus as he's deid, which says tae me that someone was tryin' tae cover their tracks. As for the lack ay forced entry, well, who's tae say he just forgot tae lock the door. Ye cannae tell me ye've never done that before."

"Fair enough. But if someone was tryin' tae cover their tracks they didnae try very hard, which says tae me that they didnae try at aw. Ah mean why bother tae dae ay half clean up job? Look, Ah'm just sayin' this may no be murder. Dae ye think that's possible or no?"

Williamson had another look at the room. "Oh, it's certainly possible. It's just no likely. Ah mean where are these two individuals anyway? They could've done ay runner for aw we know. Ah'm going wi ma gut instincts on this one. Ah've been daein' this work for many years now, and Ah may very well be gettin' close tae retirement sae that Ah can make way for the next generation ay T.V. style detectives, but Ah'll tell ye something, Ah'll never lose ma skill at rooting out mean criminal scum. Ye dinnae spend this long in the trenches without picking up certain intuitions. Putting away the bad guys is what Ah dae. Ah sleep better at night, and Ah'm goin' tae jail a couple more before Ah pack it aw in!" Williamson sneered just before slapping his hand down hard on the bodybag containing Raymond's corpse. "Jesus fuckin' Christ! What is he still daein'

67

here? God, Parker, he's only been deid a day or two and already he stinks like a bloody turd. Hey, will somebody please take him outta the van! Where the hell did the coroner go for God's sake! He shoulda been bagged and tagged hours ago! You, aye you! Wakey, wakey! Go get someone!" Williamson then continued as he gestured angrily to a passing officer to find out what was going on.

Parker, however, wasn't convinced. To him it didn't feel like murder. Something was missing. He just couldn't put his finger on exactly what it was. "They're just students. There's nae concrete evidence here tae suggest foul play or criminal activity," he added.

"Oh really? Think, Parker. Ye found the bag ay marijuana yersel! They're fuckin' stoners for cryin' out loud! God alone knows what they're capable ay."

"Smokin' a wee bit weed doesnae make ye a killer. That's a tad excessive," Parker chuckled, dismissing Williamson as he again tried to put the brakes on his overzealousness.

"Now yer startin' tae sound like one ay they hippies."

"Hardly. Anyway, we'll know more after the autopsy. In the meantime Ah guess we should find these tae characters and see what, if anything, they know."

"Oh, Ah guarantee they two know sommit. Ah'm tellin' ye. Nine times outta ten the victim either knows or is related tae whomever perpetrated the crime. Besides, we've interviewed aw his neighbours and nobody knows or seems tae huv seen anything. Very suspicious if ye ask me. Someone went tae great lengths tae make sure they weren't seen."

Parked nodded in acknowledgement. "Yeah, but judging from upstairs ye'd be forgiven for thinking the lads' flat had been ransacked anaw. It's sae hard tae tell. How could anyone purposely live like that?"

"Aye, it beggars belief."

"Ah think we should question the gas man who found the body again. See if we can jog his memory. There must be something else. He said he arrived first thing this morning tae service the boiler but there was nae answer. Sae he returned around noon only tae find the door ajar. Sae we huv tae separate occasions where he could've seen somebody or something outta the ordinary," Parker reasoned.

"Okay, but Ah think yer wasting yer time. Ah think we both know what happened here," said Williamson. His mind was made up long ago.

"We also gotta pay another visit tae the taxi rank down the street. We huvnae interviewed aw the drivers yet. And if that place is open twenty-four seven, then that helps us fill in our time frame. Because if there was a window of opportunity then we need tae narrow it down," Parker said, again scribbling notes down on his pad.

"Well, Ah personally believe that we should cast the net far and wide on this one. Those two junkie bastards know sommit, Ah can feel it in ma water. Ah wanna pass on their details tae aw our colleagues and see what comes up. And Ah want their photos at every train station, ferry terminal and every airport just in case they try and leave the country on a wee holiday. We could huv a real pair ay dangerous desperados on our hands, Parker. Fugitives from the law!" Williamson barked as he again signalled an officer over before handing him the pictures they'd found.

"Let's no get ahead ay oursels. We huv other avenues tae explore remember."

"Parker, Ah gotta say Ah'm surprised at ye. We gotta collar these two. And the longer we leave it, the harder it'll be," urged Williamson.

"And we will. Ah'm just sayin' ye think this is a murder scene. But the fact is we dinnae know the cause ay death for certain yet. Ye might very well turn out tae be right, but at present yer jumpin' the gun. Ah think that it'd be wise tae keep this low key until we know more. The last thing we wanna do is create panic in the local area, or worse still for the press tae get a hold ay this. Imagine if they prick's found out. It would be a wee bit embarrassing tae huv tae dae a public U-turn. All cos we got it wrong and wanted tae change our minds. Look, we could post an officer outside the premises here. Ah'm sure Mr Townsend and Mr Majors will turn up sooner or later, probably hungover from some all-night rave or sommit."

"Jesus Christ, Parker! Wake up and look around! Dinnae be sae naïve. This isnae right. Why take that chance?" Williamson raged. His patience had run out.

69

Chapter 8

Now aboard the aircraft Morgan and Stuart fought their way through the maelstrom to their respective seats.

"Look, Ah nae woosy. Ah'd just rather sit by the window if that's okay wi ya?" fretted Morgan.

Stuart grudgingly obliged and let Morgan in first. "Fine, whatever. We huvnae got aw day."

"Excuse me. But I'd rather sit by the window if it's all the same to you," said a strangely familiar voice. It was the creepy gentleman dressed in black from the departure lounge.

"Well, that settles that. Aye, Ah'm sure that'd be fine, pal," Stuart said, standing to one side.

Morgan's face fell like an avalanche when he realised who it was. "Nice one, silly bollocks. God, Ah dinnae believe this. Thanks a lot, Stuart." he then muttered. The thought of spending ten odd hours sat next to that guy was not something Morgan relished.

"What? He's just an old dude. He has seniority over ya. He's probably got some sort ay medical reason for wantin' tae sit by the window. Ye dinnae. Yer just gay. Ah mean, look at him. He looks half off his tits, man. Like wasted. Dinnae worry, ye'll still be fairly close tae the window," Stuart whispered to Morgan as they let the man in beside them.

Morgan forced a fake smile, but it couldn't be more insincere. "No, Ah think not! Ye can sit next tae him. Cos Ah'm taking the aisle seat."

"Make up yer bloody mind! My ex-girlfriend could make a decision faster than ya. And she was a complete neurotic nut job."

"Oh aye, Ah remember her. Whatever happened between ya tae again?" Morgan then asked, but in hindsight perhaps shouldn't have given the raw feelings Stuart still harboured toward her.

"Fuck knows? She dumped me and broke ma heart intae a million pieces, Ah'll tell ya that much"

"Ah remember that right enough. Ya were a total mess."

"She was ma sunshine dude. Ah really loved her. But apparently Ah'm a 'complete loser who'll never achieve anything.' Her words, no mine."

"Ouch, that's pretty brutal man." Morgan groaned.

"Aye, she is that. She really changed. And suffice to say, no for the better. Ah just didnae recognise her toward the end. And she soon moved on tae. Met some total dickhead. Cannae mind his name. Who cares. Good luck tae him Ah say. He'll need it. She could fall out and pick ay fight wi her own shadow. And Ah dare say he'll find out the hard way, as Ah did, that she's no the 'little Miss innocent' she potrays."

"Sounds tae me like yer better off pal."

"Aye." Stuart then sighed.

"Sae, eh? Hey, Ah must admit this is aw very exciting. Ah mean, this is insane. Ah've never been tae America before. We're actually daein' this. Beats sitting at home that's for sure," Morgan said, the reality of what they were embarking on now beginning to sink in as he tried to move on from Stuart's failed relationship.

"Aye, me neither. Sae, what are we gonna dae tae fill in our time until we get there?"

"Eh, Ah dunno? Sleep, maybe watch an inflight movie or two. Eat, sleep, listen tae the radio, drink, read, sleep. Oh, and we change planes at Washington DC."

"Why change planes? What wrong wi this one?!" Stuart panicked.

"Oh ma God! Yer right. Ah never thought ay that. We better get off!"

Stuart's face was now filled with alarm. "Dae ye think?"

"Nah, Ah'm just pullin' yer leg. It's nae different from changing trains or sommit like that. Relax."

"Sae fun and hilarity aw the way then?" Stuart sighed with relief.

Morgan nodded. "Indeed. Just like yer average day really. Well, everything apart from the winnin' the lottery and travellin' tae America tae track down a long-lost uncle ye never knew ye had bit. Other than that it's practically identical."

"Sir. I think that you're in the wrong seat. If you'll please gather your belongings and follow me," an air hostess asked as she signalled to the stranger.

"Oh, I'm so sorry, my dear. My mistake. I'll maybe see you boys around," the man grumbled, turning to Morgan and Stuart as he again squeezed past them.

"Okay, Ah'll look forward to that. Like Ah would if Ah were tae huv acupuncture done on ma scrotum," Morgan remarked, but only when he was safely out of earshot.

"What's yer problem wi him? He's just some random old fart," Stuart pointed out once again.

Morgan laughed. "Is he though? Is he really?

"Err? Aye."

"Yeah, just an old fart. Who also just happens tae be a total mentalist."

"What? Bollocks! Ye dinnae huv a Scooby who he is. Ye should learn tae be a wee bit more sociable and outgoing an' that. Ye know? Be more understanding and open tae others." Stuart suggested.

"Okay, Oprah. Anyway, this comin' from you? Ye hardly ever leave the flat, ye hermit bastard. Look, Ah'm tellin' ye. Just trust me on this. Ah'm serious. Ah thought he was dying or sommit back in the departure lounge. Then he started spoutin' out some really weird dark pish before going on tae tell me the world is actually run by goblins. Ah dunno? There's just sommit about him. Call it a vibe. It really unnerved me," Morgan confessed.

Stuart just shrugged his shoulders. "Goblins? Sae he's a bit ay a loon ye think? Ah cannae say Ah really noticed tae be honest."

"Yes, Ah dae! He gave me the heebee fuckin' geebee's, alright? The real creeps, man. And Ah'm delighted not tae be sittin' next tae him, put it that way." Morgan shivered.

Just then the aircraft lurched into life and began to taxi down the runway. It moved slowly at first but soon gathered momentum as the engines increased in volume until the rumble from the wheels on the tarmac ceased and it took to the air.

Chapter 9

Karl, Steve and Marcus had long since left Rico Leony's beach house and had made their way to San Francisco. Their main reason for going there was that they needed supplies and information. They had a local unofficial office where they stored tracking and surveillance equipment along with possible leads as to Lawrence's probable whereabouts. Their only other clues were taken from details written down by Mr Leony himself, and the information gleaned there was scant to say the least. Yet this is what they were paid to do. After all, they were professionals and they'd done this kind of job a thousand times before. Karl and Marcus especially being as they were the veterans of the trio. With a combined fifty odd years of experience in the field between them, both had extensive military training and a history in assisting with many governmental contracts and black ops missions, this usually in conjunction with the Federal Bureau of Investigation and federal task forces including the Central Intelligence Agency. Steve, however, was just a kid when they first met. He was the younger brother of John Hickman, John being an original member and leader of their little outfit but he was shot dead in a job that went south some years back. It wasn't long after his funeral that Steve stumbled across some of his older brother's personal belongings. Suffice to say this was highly sensitive and incriminating material. Steve knew pretty much everything from that moment on. Well, he knew enough. Enough to totally compromise their entire operation. What were Karl and Marcus to do? They couldn't kill him, not that was ever an option. They'd sworn to look out for Steve on John's deathbed. They had no choice but to bring him in which coincidentally, and more than a little ironically, was also something they promised they'd never do. John had always tried to shield Steve from that side of his life and with more than adequate reason. However, this was seen to be the lesser of two evils, and at least this way they could keep an eye on him.

Ultimately these guys were trained by us. By our government. By the very people we elect and swear into power. The very same people who in turn vow to protect us, whether that be from threats foreign or domestic. And rest assured there's always a threat, manufactured or otherwise. It doesn't really matter. There's no profit in peace. Presidents' positions need to be reinforced, military contracts must be met, spending budgets justified, overseas interests monitored and global assets such as oil seized. This is usually done under the guise of freedom, peace and democracy, not only that but it's all funded using our taxes. Nonetheless, times change or at least the customers do. The balance of power has shifted. No longer is the world run by a country's elected leader or the elite few, the world is governed by big business, shady organisations and the criminal underworld. It's a free market and there's big money to be made. These days Marcus, Steve and Karl were purely freelance and a large percentage of their business came primarily from a small group of very lucrative private contracts like Mr Leony who could afford them. Yet it wasn't too long ago that they'd have been paid to take down such individuals, the irony of which wasn't lost on them. Still, if the money was right they did the work, no questions asked. In this instance Mr Leony had stressed just how important this was. It was his mother after all, so it had already become extremely personal and no price was too high. Rico Leony had a long and colourful history of being the type of man who gets what he wants, this usually backed up and reinforced by a very explosive temper. That said, it wasn't in his best interest to kill people that he was upset with or who got in his way personally, that just wasn't smart or good for business. He was the boss and if you take out the head the body dies. Besides, he wasn't stupid. He didn't get to where he was today by running around like *Rambo*. He didn't have to. He had people to take care of the uglier, more unpleasant side of things. Expendable people. That's not to say that he never got his hands dirty. Far from it. There are always exceptions from the rules, the kind of exceptions that demand to be made an example of. It's about fear and respect. It was this violent temperament that killed his wife and her young lover. When he can home early one day to find them in the throes of passion, he flipped, as you'd expect. Surprisingly, the young lover Rico could almost understand. But not forgive. He just wasn't the forgiving type. It wasn't in his nature, but he understood that he was just a dumb horny kid who didn't know any better. His wife on the other hand really should have. Her infidelity would not go unpunished, so he imprisoned both in his garage where he went to work on them using an assortment of everyday DIY power tools. This included a set of pliers, an electric belt sander and a nail gun, not to mention a seemingly innocuous bag of rock salt. An utterly horrific ordeal that he managed to stretch out for two or three days before he eventually disposed of them using no less than an industrial wood chipper. He'd always joked that his wife was full of shit and that he'd be better off using her to fertilise his garden. Well, call it fate. He didn't kill many but when he did, stand back! There really was no limit to his psychotic imagination where revenge was concerned. This was perhaps the best indication to what lay in wait for Lawrence if Rico ever caught up with him.

"Excuse me, buddy, but I don't ever remember it taking this long to get downtown. We shoulda been there by now. What's the hold up, Mr Wong or whatever your name is? Are you lost, my friend?" Steve indicated impatiently to the cab driver.

The driver looked back at Steve in his rear-view mirror. "No! And I Mr Wang!"

"Well, excuse me all the hell. Wong, Wang? Who gives a shit? Close enough," Steve replied curtly, instantly dismissing Wang's correction.

"I thought you tourist folk would appreciate extended tour round beautiful city. See sights and whatnot. Is such a glorious day. Where you from anyway?" Wang asked.

"Did you hear that? Goddamned son-of-a-bitch bastard cabbie called me a fucking tourist," Steve whispered to Karl before he went on to put the guy in his place. "Look, douchbag! Scew the fucking weather, this fucking city and all the fucking people in it! And that includes you, asshole! I'm for right here as well you know! So stop yanking my chain! Where the fuck are you from, Chinaman?"

"China."

"Well yeah, exactly. So cut the horseshit! I ain't in the mood. Tourist my ass," Steve said as he pulled out his pistol and started to wave it around in the back seat as if it were a baton and he was conducting his own orchestra of anger.

"Do you kliss your mother with that mouth?" Wang joked, but was only adding fuel to the fire.

"Do I kliss my mother with that mouth? It's kiss, dipshit. And you leave my mother outta this. You hear?!" Steve fumed.

"Look, I sorry, tough guy. I not about to argue with extra from *Saturday Night Fever.*"

"What you mean by that?"

"You guys are dressed pretty sharp. Where's the party? Ha, ha!" the cab driver replied, laying on the sarcasm good and thick, still completely unaware he was goading a hired assassin who by then was frantically pointing a gun at the back of his head.

Karl grabbed the gun from Steve. "Jesus Christ, Steve. Enough! Put that away! Besides, if you shoot him there's the very distinct possibility of us crashing this cab. And none us want that. Think, damn it!"

"Smart assed…" Steve grumbled as he settled back into his seat.

Karl looked over to the front passenger side of the cab to where Marcus was sleeping like a baby. "Hey, sleeping beauty. Wake up! We're almost there."

Moments later, "Hahhhh! Okay, girls. We here. End of line. That'll be thirty dollar!" the driver announced, only adding further tension to an already delicate situation.

Karl grudgingly passed the driver the fare. "I may shoot that thieving Jap bastard myself. Fucking daylight robbery. We're in the wrong business," he said turning to Steve.

"It ain't too late," Steve acknowledged, as he reached inside his jacket as if going for his piece.

"Ha, ha, ha! I told you. I thieving Chinese bastard, honky!" the driver cackled.

"Whatever!" both Karl and Steve echoed.

"Who? What?" asked Marcus who came to just as the cab screeched to a halt.

"Ah, you've decided to join us at long last. I was going to leave you here and let you enjoy the extended tourist tour. Running commentary and all," said Karl.

"What?"

"Nothing. Come on."

76

Steve had already left the taxi and made his way towards their office closely followed by Karl who'd left Marcus standing at the side of the road trying to light a cigarette. Each attempt to successfully strike a match, however, failed much to his frustration.

"Screw this! I was gonna quit anyway," Marcus told himself out loud as he abandoned his cigarette to follow his two colleagues.

The office they had was no bigger than a few medium-sized rooms. Two of those rooms were just like your average business with all the usual paraphernalia you'd expect, computers, phones, photocopier and fax machine, all of which were functioning and used daily. Just not by them. They all served as the perfect front for their base however. The third and in fact largest room was used to store the aforementioned weaponry, intelligence files, surveillance equipment and the like. There really was quite the arsenal hidden from view. The place itself, or at least the name above the door, was a family ties agency. It was part of a global network much like the one used by Stuart to find Lawrence. All the names of people who want a relation or loved one found are entered into a computer database, one of which was in the office. Anything keyed into a computer in say New York or indeed Britain becomes available on every office outlet to keep up links with one another. So this had become the ideal place to conceal a list of names of people due for assassination. It was a legitimate business with a real secretary who knew nothing of their true involvement in the running of things. She sure as hell didn't know about the small arms room sitting right under her nose. Margaret, their secretary, believed Karl, Steve and Marcus were nothing more than travelling company employees involved in the marketing between each of the outlets. The only reason the trio got involved in this whole affair was through a mutual friend, Harvey, who was once in the same line of work as they are in now. However, he got arrested by police after he'd tried to kill someone who'd stolen his client's jewels during an armed heist that went sideways right here in San Francisco. Harvey now managed the agency thanks to a few pulled strings courtesy of none other than Mr Leony. That way Harvey could appear to be keeping his nose clean while at the same time still help out when required.

Margaret was working away feverishly at her desk as she always did due to the fact that she was the only one who ever did anything. Harvey was asleep, or taking an 'executive nap' as he would put it, in the next room.

Karl was first in as he barged his way past Steve. "Where the hell is Harvey?" he then asked Margaret abruptly.

Margaret, who was trying desperately to get through her mountain of paperwork despite her nipping arthritis, didn't even hear them enter.

"HELLO! Anybody there?" Karl bellowed as he slammed his hand down on the desk in a bid to get her attention.

The poor woman nearly dropped dead of a heart attack right there and then. "Oh my Lord!" she gasped.

Karl forced a fake smile. "No. Not quite. Maybe next time. Harvey, where is he? Is he asleep through the back again?"

Margaret took a moment to compose herself. "Yes, I believe so. Nice to see you again, Mr Sharp."

"You believe so? Either he is or he isn't. It's a yes, no question, lady! Christ, give me strength!" Karl snapped as he made his way to the next room.

Steve followed close behind. "Sorry about him. He's pretty highly strung at times. Just between you and me, I think it's the male menopause or something. Marcus is no better. I've been stuck with those two for way too long now. They bicker like an old cranky married couple," he said in an attempt to comfort her after Karl's less than polite entrance.

"Okay, that's it! I've had it. No more cigarettes. They're killing me. I can't breathe and I'm so pissed off. Every match in the entire box either broke or blew out. Can you believe that, man? God, I'm dying for a smoke," Marcus babbled as the door flew open behind Steve.

"See what I mean, Margaret? Marcus, you might, and this is just a suggestion so don't bite my head off here, but you might wanna think about investing in a windproof lighter. Like a Zippo? I don't think it's your cigarettes or matches that are to blame. Oh, wait! Or better still, join the twenty-first century and get one of those e-cigarettes. You should be vaping. People are going for those in a big way," Steve suggested.

"Are you sure about that, Columbo? Listen, I'm well aware of all of what you say. I have, or rather had, a Zippo but fucking lost it. E-cigarettes? I dunno? Maybe. Is it a real substitute though? Why are all the best things bad for you?" Marcus acknowledged.

"You said it yourself. Cigarettes will kill you. Those electronic ones won't. It's a positive selling point. And there's gum and patches too. There's no excuse. That's gotta be worth considering, surely?"

"It's too late for me to worry about all that now. I just need to find myself a new vice," Marcus insisted.

"What like whores or crack?" laughed Steve.

"I was thinking more along the lines of coffee, Steve. A large, strong black coffee. That'd work," answered Marcus as he made his way to the coffee machine in the corner of the room.

Karl stood in the back office where he'd found Harvey. "Hey, you lazy fat ape! Get up!"

"Ahhh? Err? I guess I might've fallen asleep waiting for you guys. What took you so long anyway?" Harvey then asked as he pulled himself up off the desk that he'd been sprawled across.

"A little yellow man in a little yellow car," Karl grumbled.

"What?"

"Never mind. Best not get into that now. I don't wanna set Steve off again. I swear that kid's nuts. He just acts on pure impulse and it makes him very unpredictable. He's a fucking liability at times, or maybe I'm just getting old."

"Steve's a character for sure. He actually reminds me of a younger you." Harvey nodded.

"Yeah, maybe. Anyway, I couldn't help but notice that a certain old bitch is still employed here. You should get rid of her. Part exchange her for a fitter model. This place needs some eye candy, seriously. Someone with big tits and a tight ass would be a good start," Karl mused.

"Margaret?"

"Well, I ain't talking about you!"

"I think you protest too much about her. I think there might be something there. It could be beautiful."

79

"Fuck you. I'm old but I'm not that old."

Harvey laughed. "Well, I did tell her that if she didn't get her shit together she was out. She, of course, gave me this long drawn out sob story about how she needs the money. You know, to hold on to her house and keep her kids in school or whatever. But I just told her to take it up with someone who gives a rat's ass. I don't know how much longer she can hack it. Not that I'd seriously get rid of her you understand. I just say that shit for my own amusement. It's hilarious. I've never seen such pathetic desperation. Besides, it helps keep me sane but perhaps more importantly it gives her the fear. She works like a maniac. She does all the work. It's great. I ain't done shit in months," he then conceded.

"You sick twisted bastard. And don't worry, I can see that you ain't exactly knocking yourself out here. Wait, she's got kids? Is that possible? Is it legal? I mean, she must weigh about the same as my fucking Buick. And how old is she anyway? Not to mention some poor prick, no pun intended, would have to... you know?" Karl said and was dumbfounded.

"That dried-up old wench? Hardly. She adopted no-hopers from off the streets and they rob her blind. But as she says, 'they're my little rascals'," Harvey revealed as he raised his eyes to the ceiling.

A look of pure evil came across Karl's face. "They're gonna kill her, aren't they?"

"God, I hope not. I might actually have to do some work around here. I don't even know how to turn my computer on for Christ's sake. I hate it here, man. I need to get back in the game. I ain't cut out for this shit. A case in point. Thanks to me we accidentally mismatched thousands of our clients meaning there's now a lot of folk out there who are gonna be wrongly paired up with a complete stranger who has nothing to do with them whatsoever. Still, what's the worst that can happen, right?" Harvey admitted.

"Woops! So watcha gonna do?" Karl sniggered.

"Are you kidding me? I ain't saying squat. If it comes back on me, you know who I'm blaming. Failing that my plan B is to, I dunno? Sell a kidney or win the lotto. Which reminds me that I didn't get one damned number last night. Not one. That's like the third or fourth consecutive time. Some lucky son-of-a-bitch did

80

though. Scooped the entire jackpot. But they ain't come forward yet. Why the hell not? What possible reason could you have? Although, imagine you lost the ticket. I'd be fucking suicidal."

"Yeah, that would be a total head fuck," Karl acknowledged as Marcus joined them with his polystyrene cup of coffee in hand.

"Quit your dreaming, Harv. They say statistically you've got more chance of being struck by lightning, if you can believe that. Anyway, I've been meaning to ask you. Did you ever catch up with that Terry character you were so pissed off with?" Marcus then asked switching the subject.

"Hey, don't even talk to me about that asshole. I'm never going to fully retire until he's dead. I've got one bullet left with his name on it. Motherfucker ran me over and damn near paralysed my ass!" Harvey fumed.

"Face facts, Harv. You got sloppy and you got fucked. Anyway, did you get all the stuff we requested?" Marcus asked in an attempt to get down to business, but after his blunt comment that was very unlikely.

"Yeah, of course. What do you take me for? And listen, my shit is as tight as ever. That clown shouldn't have been given a licence to drive in the first place. He came outta nowhere. He shoulda been looking where he was going," Harvey said in an attempt to defend himself.

"Stop, look and listen, man. You were fucking jay walking. You learn this shit in kindergarten," Marcus said poking fun at Harvey's expense.

"Same old Marcus. 'Mr Perfect.' Fuck me, do you ever stop?"

"That's funny you say that cos your mom said almost those exact words to me last night," Marcus said as he continued to mock Harvey.

"You know I ain't shot no one in a while. I wonder if my gun still works? Perhaps you'd like to swallow a little lead," Harvey asked as he pretended to shoot Marcus with his gun.

"Wow! You can come on to me all you want with your seedy sexual innuendos, but it won't get you anywhere. I ain't one of your fun boys, ha, ha!" Marcus laughed.

81

"Back the fuck off, man. I know what this is about. I didn't know it was that kinda bar, alright! Thanks, Karl. I told you that in confidence," Harvey informed Marcus before turning his attention to Karl.

"Sorry, Harv. It just sorta slipped out." Karl sniggered.

"Come on. The Blue Oyster? And you didn't have to stay there for nearly half an hour," Marcus continued and could hardly keep the smile from his face.

"Look, I didn't wanna be rude. And the music was actually pretty good," insisted Harvey.

"Ha, ha, ha! Look, if you prefer bum there ain't nobody here judging. Times have changed. It's cool, man. Don't hide away and live a life of shame and denial. We're all friends here," Karl replied, now getting in on the joke.

"You know what? Fuck this, fuck that and fuck you man! And yeah, we are friends. And if you want things to remain that way I suggest you drop it. For the sake of general peace and harmony I'm willing to let that slide. But enough is enough. Agreed?" Harvey said laying down a curt ultimatum.

"Agreed," Karl acknowledged.

Marcus also nodded in agreement. "Yeah, me too. Sorry, Harv. You'd do the same though."

"So who's 'Mr Unlucky' this time?" Harvey wondered, relieved to be moving on.

Marcus pulled up a seat opposite Harvey. "You won't believe it but some absolute retard managed to burn Rico Leony's mansion to the ground and…"

"You're kidding me?" Harvey interjected.

"Wait, it gets better," Karl added.

"Yeah, the only thing is Rico's mom was in the house at the time," Marcus continued.

"No way!"

Marcus looked puzzled. "So you've heard none of this?"

"Well, I know some. It was all over the news. You couldn't very well miss it. But I heard it was an accidental fire. I certainly didn't know somebody deliberately torched the place and his mom too!

That's fucked up! Talk about signing your own death warrant," Harvey said, still shocked by these new revelations.

"We actually don't know for sure if the fire was accidental or deliberate," Karl conceded.

"Hey, now you're talking semantics. The bottom line is she's fucking toast. Rico's about to go supernova and we've been given the task of finding the jerk-off who's responsible. Not to mention the fact he shouldn't have been there in the first instance. The piece of shit was trying to rob the place, for crying out loud. And that's a fact," Marcus stressed.

"How is Rico anyway? I've not had the nerve to phone him yet. It seems too soon. I'll send him a card with my condolences," said Harvey.

Karl pulled up a third chair. "Suffice to say he's furious. And believe me that's probably the understatement of the century. How would you feel?"

There followed a short pause. "Who did it?" Harvey said, asking the obvious next logical question.

"Some screw up waste of space called Lawrence Lowmax. He was in the movie business. Now it seems he just cons his way into people's lives before ripping them off," Karl revealed.

"The movies? Really? What was he an actor or something? What films has he done?"

"That's what I asked. An innocent enough question you would've thought. But no," Steve said as he stood in the doorway while tucking into a bag of homemade cookies Margaret had given him.

"Steve, there's a time and a place for what you said and it was neither the time nor the place, the major difference being Rico not standing right there as you were asking it. We've been through all this. You're just damn lucky Rico didn't crucify your ass there and then," Karl pointed out.

"And I apologised for that. Quite living in the past, Karl. Move on," Steve muttered.

"So what films did he do then?"

"Fuck's sake! I dunno, Harv? Like I said to Steve, I didn't get his portfolio. I just know he worked in that business for a time. In make-up and special effects, I think."

"So not an actor then?"

"I guess not, no!" Karl sighed in utter exasperation.

"So anyway. Wheels, did you get..." Marcus began in a bid to get back on track.

"My God! Have you tried these cookies? Mmmm! Mmmm! Yummy. They're dangerously good," Steve interrupted as he offered the bag around.

Nobody answered Steve as Marcus continued. "Have you arranged transport..." but he was again stopped mid sentence.

"Do you want one or..." Steve wasn't allowed to finish this time.

"If you don't shut the hell up, Steve, I swear I'm gonna stuff that whole bag down your pain in the ass throat!" Marcus warned Steve.

"Jees, no need to get all bent outta shape about it. What flew up your ass anyway?" whinged Steve.

"Nothing, but I guarantee something hard, black and leathery is going to shoot up yours if you butt in one more time!" Marcus threatened Steve for the last time.

Thankfully Harvey intervened. "I got you a Jeep. It's nothing fast or flash. You wanted something inconspicuous, right? And more importantly it's reliable and has enough room for any supplies or dead bodies that will undoubtedly accumulate."

Marcus loosened his tie. "It ain't hot, is it? Cos I don't want to get pulled over by the boys in blue like what happened a few jobs back. I had to cash in more than just a favour or two that day, I can tell you."

"No, it's cleaner than a bar of soap. It ain't even picked up a parking ticket," Harvey assured Marcus before throwing him the keys.

"Then let's get to work." Marcus added.

84

Chapter 10

Meanwhile, flying somewhere over the Atlantic Ocean: "What the blazes? Bloody typical!" Stuart began.

"What now?"

"Ah only got one packet ay sugar wi me tea. That's the equivalent ay one teaspoon, if even that. What if yer a two sugars man? What then, eh? Stingy bastards. It's like they take ye halfway there only tae stop dead and drop ya off in the middle ay nowhere," Stuart moaned bitterly.

Morgan passed Stuart his unused sugar. "Here, have mine. Problem solved. Case closed. Move on."

"Problem nae solved. Case ongoing. There's a principle at stake here, dude," Stuart insisted.

"Fuck's sake! It's like going on a holiday wi a five-year old. Yer hyperactive, man. The one thing ye dinnae need is more sugar. Ye havnae stopped wittering on for hours now. Besides, sugar's bad for ya," Morgan barked.

"Ah'm a smoking, binge drinkin' habitual drug user. Dae ye really think Ah'm bothered by the amount ay sugar Ah consume?" Stuart pointed out.

"Well, maybe ya should be. Obesity, diabetes, poor oral health. Need Ah go on?"

"Please dinnae. What are ya, a walkin' talkin' government health pamphlet? And sae what if Ah'm a wee bit hyper. Ah'm excited. What in the hell is wrong wi you anyway? Anybody would think it was yer time ay the month or sommit, ye big girl. And just why on earth would ya be going on holiday wi a five-year old anyway by the way? Ya pervert. There's a name for people like you. And a register anaw."

"Aye, Ah know. Pervert, ya just said it."

"Ah, sae ya admit it then."

"No! That's no what Ah meant and ya know it. God, ye'd drive even the saintliest person tae the brink ay utter despair, ya know that."

"Now yer comparing yersel tae a saint? Well, someone's got an awfully inflated opinion ay themselves. A pervert transformed tae a saint in the blink ay an eye. It's a classic story. Ah gotta say ya've really turned yer life around."

"AHHH! Piss off! Yer really starting tae grate ma cheese."

"What's wrong really, chief? Cos it isnae the amount ay sugars in ma tea. And if it is, well, that's hardly much ay an issue on the grand scale ay things. Besides yer nae ma mother."

Morgan looked at the mess around them. "If ye cast yer mind back ye'll recall the state ay the flat and the absolute obscenity ya created there."

"Oh, yeah. The flat ruled."

"Good, now hold on tae that memory. Now, Ah'm just curious but is it some kinda primal instinct that ye feel ye must recreate yer favoured living environment? Kinda like yer natural habitat. Or maybe ye can explain how and why in the space ay a few short hours ye huv single handily brought the same look and smell ay the flat intae our already cramped space. Ah mean, look at the rubbish that ya huv amassed. If it wasnae sae disgusting Ah'd almost be impressed. Oh, and by the way, the first few packets ay peanuts and tins ay beer are complimentary. After that ya pay. What ya dinnae dae is swipe stuff off the trolley when she isnae looking. That's stealing. It must run in the family or something. Yer uncle is a compulsive liar and... and a felon. And you, yer a kleptomaniac for Christ's sake."

"Err? What were the choices again? Sorry, dude, Ah completely zoned out there," Stuart asked, lost in a mixture of confusion and boredom.

Morgan folded up his table and turned to Stuart, "Choices? What are ya talkin' about? Ah was simply stating ay matter ay fact. Oh, and ya know what else has been bothering me while we're on the subject?"

"No. But if Ah can just address the whole snack food issue for a sec. Why the hell does the complimentary nachos and tins ay beer as ya call em' huv tae be sae small? Why would making things smaller be better? Ah mean, since when was calling something 'fun size' deemed tae be mair fun? Where's the fun in getting less? There's nae fun in that. It's like, 'here ye go, get just enough ay a taste ay yer chosen treat or beverage but no enough tae in any way satisfy ya. But enough tae get ya drooling for more like some kinda desperate junkie looking for their next fix.' Who are they trying tae kid? Fun? My arse be the way. It's an insult."

"When Ah hold those tiny novelty packets in the palm ay ma hand Ah personally find it oddly empowering. Ah like tae pretend for a moment that Ah'm some kinda giant," Morgan revealed, but looked almost embarrassed and more than a little taken aback by his own honesty.

"Aye, there's a certain amusement value in that, granted. But it's still tight though, no tae mention any entertainment derived from said activity is very quickly negated by the damn near impossibility ay opening one ay they packets in the first place. And even when ya dae most packets are half filled wi nothin' more than air." Stuart sighed before licking the last of the salt and nutty remnants out of the bottom of his tiny packet.

"Anyway, Stuart, as Ah was saying," Morgan said trying to swing the topic of conversation back around again.

"What? What's bothering ya then, Morgan?" Stuart grudgingly asked.

"My conscience and yesterday."

Stuart looked bewildered. "What, the fact that we're rich beyond our wildest dreams? Oh, Ah see. Ya think that we should donate some tae charity? Well, Ah must say that's very commendable and aw, but they scrounging scumbags can fuck right off. Ah am charity by the way."

"Yer all heart. No! The bits inbetween. Leaving Raymond deid like that and going the way we did. That kinda thing. Was it the right thing tae dae? Put it this way, a lot ay weird shit has happened and we never really once stopped tae think."

"Exactly. And what's the moral message there?"

"Ah dunno? Think ay others?"

"No. Dinnae think! It's only gonna complicate matters. And where does it get you really? It's totally overrated. Besides, who gives a flyin' monkey's toss about that thieving scabby bastard Raymond or those stupid puke eating dugs? We're rich now and we're going tae America. Sae lighten up, amigo," Stuart said, basking in the thought of his new found wealth.

"Yeah, but…"

"Save it! Ah've a bit ay a turtle heid situation going on. Sae Ah'm away tae drop the kids off at the pool," Stuart then bluntly informed Morgan.

As Stuart made his way to the toilet Morgan was left alone with his thoughts. His mind raced as he began to wonder about all that had transpired and where it was leading. Everything had happened so fast. It was now like a distant memory despite it only happening a few short hours ago. Then there was Stuart. Morgan had never seen him act like this before. He'd always been so laid-back and happy-go-lucky. He was generally unexcited or too affected by anything, yet here he was on cloud nine. The enthusiasm Morgan could understand. It appeared they'd just won the lottery after all. It was the ruthless streak and greedy glint in Stuart's eye that didn't sit well with Morgan. He'd really changed and he wasn't even rich yet. The very thought seemed to be enough. Morgan was also all too aware of the amount of time they'd be spending together in close proximity. It was going to be twenty-four seven living in one another's pockets. Sure, they were flatmates, but this would be a whole other level which can put a strain on any relationship no matter how strong. Morgan had a life outside the flat and Stuart. If he wasn't at college he was out with mates grabbing a pint or doing the everyday mundane things like getting in the shopping. Stuart was like the couch or television. He was part of the fixtures and fittings. Morgan couldn't actually recall the last time he'd been alone in the flat. Morgan wasn't even altogether sure what Stuart actually did. If he was still a student then Morgan didn't know for sure what it was he was meant to be studying. If he ever quizzed Stuart on the subject he'd mutter something about chemistry which Morgan began to wonder maybe closer to the truth then Stuart had intended given his obvious current vocation. The bottom line was that Morgan was beginning to feel a little unsure of their entire situation. Yes, he wanted the money. Who wouldn't? But just how far were they willing to go to get it? And what would it do to them when they did? Stuart just didn't seem too bothered by yesterday's events. Morgan by contrast was feeling racked with guilt, particularly for the way they had treated Mr Lucus. Okay, he wasn't exactly Raymond's number one fan, far from it, but he knew what they did was wrong. Then what about Lawrence? Morgan couldn't trust anyone he didn't know. Not completely at any rate. Especially when that person also happened to be a convicted criminal. That said, he did send the lotto ticket, so at least that much had checked out. Then there was one last thing. Stuart had no family. Well, not until 'uncle' Lawrence had arrived on the scene. Could his overwhelming desire for a family be so strong that it would blind him and ultimately impair his better judgement?

Stuart by comparison was having his own problems, albeit a tad more one dimensional. Sitting on the toilet he'd become all too aware of his very cramped and claustrophobic surroundings, and he'd just released in a sort of pre-emptive warning shot to the full scale event of some particularly noxious gas. Like some kind of venting volcano before its inevitable eruption. The air was thick with a heavy sulphurous stench that you could've cut with a knife. It was so pungent that he could almost taste it, and it's not as if he could open a window. Of course, if Stuart were to be optimistic he could simply walk away complaining of the smell and so diverting the obvious finger of shame from himself. But realistically that was never going to work. The last person to leave always gets the blame, so why would this be any different? Besides, he'd been in there long enough and there was bound to be a queue waiting to get in. Still, it wasn't as if he hadn't faced this kind of situation before. In different circumstances maybe, but the rules were exactly the same. The only sure fire way out of the dilemma come nightmare scenario was to do the business while staying firmly fixed to the toilet, thus preventing the offensive odour full access to the plane's atmosphere. So Stuart sat welded to the toilet and flushed while remaining perfectly in position. It worked and almost too well as he was also very nearly vacuumed from the aircraft. He felt his bowels give an almighty heave as the contents of the toilet bowl were instantly sucked away by the single most horrendous noise he'd ever heard. This exacerbated by the fact that said noise had a direct correlation with the pain in his backside. Talk about shitting one's self twice. Stuart only just managed to prise his bum cheeks from off the toilet seat before his anus, intestines, stomach and God only knows what else were wrenched out of his arse. It was enough to leave any man feeling totally violated and it showed. He was as white as a ghost and sweating profusely. It was as if he'd had to run for his very life. He tried desperately to compose himself but there was no hiding the fact that he'd suffered some kind of horrific scare.

"What happened? Ya look like yer mum just caught ya having a fly Han Solo or sommit."

"Err, Han Solo? What? Ya've gone aw *Star Wars* on me, nerd boy."

"Han Solo. Ya know, wank."

"Nice. Ah see what ya've done there. Okay, ye've probably ruined one of ma favourite *Star Wars* characters who will now forever be known as nothing more than a tosser, but that's actually quite funny for you. Ya almost took ma mind off the fact the frigging toilet's a damned death trap. No wait, ya huvnae. Cos Ah still feel cheap n' dirty. The bastard thing abused me, dude. It's practically rape. Ah should press charges," Stuart quivered nervously as he took his seat once more.

Morgan laughed. "Yeah, Ah know. The first time Ah used one Ah wasnae even needing tae go, but outta curiosity Ah hit that innocent enough lookin' wee button. After that ma body had other ideas. Although, once ya realise the deal it's actually quite ingenious. For example, if yer in a rush or just dinnae seem able tae hit target thereby spraying the toilet seat. Could be a bit ay unexpected turbulence or whatever. Embarrassment is easily avoided thanks tae the tremendous suction that ya get at these altitudes."

"Aye, maybe. Still, Ah dare say it may huv lessened the shock if ya had told me about this a little sooner."

"That's what ye would think. And in theory you'd be correct, but in practice it just doesnae work like that. A damn near heart attack is fairly inevitable Ah'm afraid. It's a baptism ay fire. Ya just gotta jump right in. Besides, Ah sure as hell wouldnae get quite the same level ay enjoyment outta it if Ah had warned ya. No tae mention huvin' this delightful wee conversation."

"Hey, Ah may very well be bored but that isnae exactly ma idea ay excitement. Ah mean, what dae ay dae up here? Ah wonder if we'd be allowed tae see the cockpit, and the pilots, and the buttons, and aw that stuff?" Stuart then said enthusiastically.

Morgan poured himself a Coke. "Ah've seen it aw before."

"Really?" Stuart said, his hopes now raised.

"Aye, Ah was eight at the time, Stuart. And dinnae go thinkin' ye'll get tae either. Ye've got zero chance. No nowadays. Cos ay terrorism and that."

Stuart snatched the rest of Morgan's Coke off him. "Ah sense that yer tryin' tae tell me somethin'. Like maybe yer tryin' tae wreck ma childhood dream. Yer such a killjoy dick!" he then snarled before promptly putting on a pair of earphones to watch the inflight movie thus preventing Morgan time to reply.

"It's nae ma fault. It's no as if Ah bombed their village, stole their oil and tried tae force democracy on them," Morgan muttered nonetheless.

Chapter 11

Prison was working out better than expected for Lawrence. The letter from the family links agency couldn't have come at a more convenient time. After spending a very painful few months in prison hospital and a further couple of months adjusting to prison life, things were finally looking up. He'd spent quite some time writing to Stuart in an attempt to build up a watertight friendship between them. Winning the lottery only confirmed Stuart's importance, mainly because he'd become his one and only realistic hope of getting the money. Unbeknown to him however, the prison board, in light of it being his first offence along with his outstanding behaviour, not to mention his unfortunate disabilities, were about to decide that he should be released. Apparently on the grounds of diminished responsibility. A technicality you might say. This of course was an unexpected and fantastic development. He'd fooled them all and had beaten the system. He'd played his hand perfectly and now he was out, a free man, well short of his intended sentence. Yet the lotto ticket was already in the prison mail and about to make its way to Stuart. Lawrence never for a second envisaged such a scenario. If he had he'd obviously never have sent it. He wouldn't have needed to. Stuart had suddenly become surplus to requirements. This was a complication that he now found himself wishing he could've avoided. His original plan had simply been to use Stuart to post his bail. With that no longer an issue he knew that he had to make some kind of attempt at intercepting it. The ticket had only been airmailed a couple of days prior, so if he had any chance of getting to it before Stuart he had to leave for Britain as soon as humanly possible. Lawrence did have one thing to his advantage. That being that Stuart knew about the win but he didn't yet know the ticket was on its way as Lawrence was only able to make phone calls out of prison on his day release pass. With his immediate freedom from incarceration very much on the horizon they'd stopped dead. Lawrence now had an entirely new plan. Assuming he was successful in reacquiring the ticket his aim was now to flee the border to Mexico. He'd already arranged the use of a fake passport but would also need some cash. Fortunately, Lawrence had an old friend, Pablo, a Mexican who owned a small bar in downtown San Francisco. Pablo was a fine upstanding gentleman, a hard-working pillar of the community who looked every bit the sixty-eight years old that he was. He'd been more of a father figure to Lawrence than anything else in the early years, always looking out for him and trying to keep him on the straight and narrow. As time passed however, their relationship seriously deteriorated. Pablo had ultimately come to realise that Lawrence would have to learn the hard way. Paying his countless debts simply hadn't worked, so he'd basically had enough and decided to wash his hands of him. In fact, Lawrence probably would've sent the ticket to Pablo if he actually thought for one second that he'd believe it and not just throw the ticket straight in the trash. So perhaps unsurprisingly Lawrence hadn't set foot in Pablo's in years. He hoped all was the same or rather that all had been forgiven and forgotten. The latter Lawrence was yet to discover. As for the place itself? Well, barring the odd crack or mark from general wear and tear it hadn't changed in the slightest. It looked just like something from straight out of an old Clint Eastwood spaghetti western. Naturally, being true to form, the food was heavily spiced to disguise its otherwise bland taste and the fact it was probably about a month old. Mercifully however the beer was far more palatable, if for no other reason than its strong alcohol content acting as a kind of sterilising agent to cleanse the pallet after whatever the hell it was you'd just eaten.

"Is that you, Pablo, you old son-of-a-gun," Lawrence asked as he entered the bar breaking the screen of cigarette smoke.

Pablo glanced over and nodded his head. "It's good to see you, Lawrence," but what he really meant was it was good to see the dumb bastard was still alive.

Lawrence made his way to the bar where he sat on a stool opposite Pablo. "I'm sorry but it's been a while," he then muttered pathetically, the guilt of his overdue absence clear for all to see.

"It has. But then you couldn't very well see me while you were locked up inside," Pablo said cutting straight to the chase. The room now filled with unexpected tension.

93

"Sorry?" Lawrence asked. How the hell did he know?

Pablo looked straight through Lawrence and his nervy smile like he wasn't even there. "Don't insult my intelligence, you stupid prick!"

"Pablo?" Lawrence spluttered out, taken aback my Pablo's directness.

"Shut up and let me finish! Prison alright, I found out you were in prison. I knew this would happen. I warned you it would. Then I hear you killed somebody's mother! What is this? And you rob a bank? What are you, outta your mind?" Pablo barked, as he pointed his finger directly in Lawrence's face.

"Err? So you heard about that then?" Lawrence asked apprehensively. This wasn't going to be as clear cut as he'd first anticipated. It was never going to be easy but this was an unexpected development and one Lawrence had no contingency plan for. It had been his hope to leave out the finer more incriminating details.

Pablo poured himself a large tequila and slammed it. "Ahhh! That's good shit. So, I get a phone call. Just like that. Outta the fuckin' blue. Cos guess what? Lawrence is in trouble and here you are. Again. My only surprise is that it's taken you this long."

"Listen, I'm out now…"

"So I see."

Lawrence looked carefully around the bar. It was almost deserted. "So how's business? Everything okay with you?" he then enquired in a vain attempt to get off the current theme.

"I get by. It's an honest living, but then I guess you wouldn't know much about that, would you? It being work in all. Anyway, cut the shit, Lawrence. You ain't here to make small talk. I sense you don't have the time nor the inclination so why don't you tell me what it is you want," Pablo said. He'd never been one for idle chit-chat, especially when he knew there was an ulterior motive at work.

"Okay, but you wouldn't believe me if I told you."

"Probably not, no. But that's what happened to the boy who called wolf one too many times. What the nursery rhyme doesn't tell you is, yes, the boy ultimately gets ignored, but it's the poor villagers who pay the price. They get fucked up by a marauding wolf. I guess what I'm saying here is I don't wanna be those villagers."

"I promise you won't," Lawrence assured Pablo.

"Go on then. Try me. I ain't had a good laugh in a while," Pablo said as he gestured Lawrence to continue.

"Okay, I'm just going to come right out with it. I... I won the lottery. I know it's crazy but that's it. I'm going straight this time."

"Bull fucking shit you did! Is this another one of your scams? It certainly ain't funny. It's ridiculous. At best it's just plain sad. Is that the best you can do? Why can't you get a proper job? Who knows, maybe even get married, settle down and have fucking kids. Even those shitty movies you used to do were better than this pathetically deluded world that you're living in now. What happened there? Oh yeah, you pissed it all away thinking you were some kinda hotshot Hollywood player. The women, the drink and the fuckin' gambling. And who baled you out time and time again? Exactly. Me. Jesus Christ, lottery? My ass. But you've really surpassed yourself this time. Murder? What the hell is that about?"

"That was an accident, alright? I didn't set out to do it. At worst it was second degree murder or something, and the truth is it was her own fault. Technically I'm an innocent man. I will admit the bank thing was a mistake. I hold my hands up there."

"Hey, a little old lady is dead, Lawrence, cos of you. So just saying 'whoops' then arguing over the technicalities don't make it right."

"She was the devil incarnate. Look, please, the only thing that stands between me and all that money is a plane fare to Britain."

"Britain? You're unbelievable. Where do you get this shit from? Are you retarded. Is it drugs? What? Whatever it is this nonsense has to stop. So you want money, do you? Well, don't tell me lies. I'm nobody's fool. I will help you. I always do. God only knows why. It clearly ain't helping, but damn it you gotta be straight with me. I mean, at the very least meet me halfway. I know you didn't win the lottery otherwise you wouldn't be asking me for money, you fucking moron! Think it through. And another thing, you're on parole. You leave the state let alone the country and they'll slap your ass back in jail quicker than it takes to have one of those prison showers."

Lawrence didn't say a word, he just gazed into Pablo's empty glass. He knew he'd let Pablo down badly this time and he wasn't

95

exactly surprised that he didn't believe a word he'd said either. It's not as if he'd ever given him good reason to.

"I will give you my passport and the money you say you need. All I ask in return is that whatever the hell it is you're up to is on the level and nobody else is gonna get hurt or, or worse," Pablo pleaded as he continued.

Lawrence couldn't even look Pablo straight in the eye. "Thank you, Pablo. I promise that I'll make all this up to you."

"No you won't. Stop making promises you can't keep."

With that Pablo went off to fetch the money and passport from his office safe through the back leaving Lawrence alone with his thoughts. Lawrence just sat there waiting and looking glumly at his reflection in the mirror behind the bar. As he did so he noticed a man standing directly behind him. The man looked at Lawrence for a second or two then left abruptly. A feeling of anxiety gripped Lawrence. It felt like the walls were suddenly closing in. Maybe it was purely because Lawrence was particularly on edge that made him so paranoid, yet he couldn't shake the suspicion that he was being shadowed. However, before he really had a chance to dwell on the matter Pablo returned.

"Here's the money. It ain't much but it's all I have. I'll be wanting my passport back though, so you get to wherever it is you're going then post it back," Pablo said.

"Thanks. Say, how did you know so much about all this anyway? I mean the bank job I understand, that's how I ended up inside, but the Mrs Leony situation? Nobody knows about that."

"I was told. The rest I investigated for myself. You see, I've had three very serious-looking guys pay me a visit on a couple of occasions. Fucking cop types only not. I couldn't say who they were for sure. Put it this way, if they were cops they were asking all the wrong questions. It just didn't make sense. Anyway, I told them nothing. I figured by the bulges in their jackets and general attitudes that they were bad news. It was obvious they wanted to have strong words with you though. And now you tell me that you're leaving the country. It can only mean one thing so go while you still can. Don't write me or call, just stay low and off the radar for a while. At least until the dust settles," Pablo warned Lawrence.

96

Lawrence got up to leave. "Okay, I gotta go. But I will see you again. Only next time I'll be the one giving you the money. We'll share a couple of cold beers and I'll explain in full this ridiculous mess," and as quickly as Lawrence had arrived he was gone, bound for the airport in a taxi.

About ten minutes later Marcus, Steve and Karl arrived looking for Lawrence. The bar door flew open as Marcus thundered in and ripped out his pistol. "WE'RE CLOSED! ANYBODY WHO AIN'T PABLO OR LAWRENCE, LEAVE NOW! Ah, there you are, Pablo. You wouldn't believe the excitement and the joy that filled my heart when I heard that little rat bastard who we've been searching for, for as long as I fuckin' care to mention, was here. And yet you didn't even have the goddamned common courtesy to give me a simple phone call. I gotta say that I'm a little hurt. Now, where is that piece of shit?" he then bellowed as he took a seat on the very same stool Lawrence had sat on moments ago.

Karl and Steve flanked Marcus left and right as they followed him in, Steve only stopping momentarily to flip the 'Open' to a 'Closed' sign on the door.

"I haven't seen him," Pablo replied, but he wasn't fooling anyone. It was written all over his face. Unlike Lawrence he'd never been much of a liar.

Marcus raised his gun into plain view and rested it on the bar right under Pablo's nose. "I think that you're lying to me, old man. And frankly that pisses me off. You know why I think you're lying? It's cos you're sweating like a pig. It ain't that hot. At least not yet. So if you've got nothing to hide why is it you look so nervous? Now tell me where he is or you may force me to lose my normally cool, calm, collected personality for something altogether more mean."

"There ain't nobody here. I told you everything I knew the last time. Either that or you guys have extremely short memories," Pablo insisted.

"Karl, check the kitchen and the alley out back. Steve, check the toilets. I'll cover our Mexican friend here," Marcus ordered as he snapped his fingers.

"Why do I have to check the toilets, man?" protested Steve.

"Cos yer a fuckin' turd alright. Now move!"

"I'm telling you, I don't know what you're talking about or what you're expecting to find."

Marcus poured himself a tequila from Pablo's bottle and slammed it before smashing the glass on the floor. "Ahhh! That'll put hair on your balls. Wrong! You see that just ain't the right answer. Now you're starting to really bore me."

"Look, I dunno what you think you know or what you've heard but I ain't seen Lawrence in years," Pablo said, again denying any knowledge of what they were asking.

"You really are quite a stubborn old son-of-a-bitch. Okay, tough guy, here's the deal. Either you tell me now what I wanna know and walk, or alternatively I have Steve over there break every single bottle from your shitty little bar over your knees. And you don't walk. Ever. Period. It's your choice," Marcus said as Steve returned from checking the toilets.

"Please, I don't know!" Pablo begged.

"There ain't nothing through there apart from the foul smell of stale piss and urinal cakes," Steve confirmed.

"Listen, we had some other addresses which we followed up. And look, I'm gonna be completely honest with you, cos you deserve to know where being purposefully obstructive will lead you. We tortured the folks concerned for information. The trouble with torture as a means of persuasion is that people will eventually pretty much tell you anything you wanna hear. It just ain't that reliable and is none too subtle either. Therefore, it's impossible to know with any degree of certainty if someone is really telling you the truth or not. And actually, to be frank, I don't think they knew a fucking thing. What I do know is if at first you don't succeed you try again, cos the law of averages dictates that sooner or later you will eventually get to the truth. That's why I'm going to keep applying pressure just to be sure, cos you gotta crack a few eggs if you wanna make an omelette. Besides, this is different. I was told by an eye witness drinking at this very same fucking shithole bar that you spoke to him only minutes ago. Explain that, motherfucker!" Marcus said as he polished his gun on the sleeve of his suit jacket.

"It's clear," Karl said as he too returned to join them.

98

"I told you, I haven't seen him. Your informant is mistaken. Anyway, you can't treat me like this. I have rights. So either piss off outta my bar or read me my rights and arrest me, cos this faggot cop routine ain't scaring me!" Pablo said, being as defiant as ever.

"Ah, Ah! I'll see your big balls and raise you. Cops? I'm sorry, who said we were cops? Who's got the poker face now? You know, I had hoped to avoid any unpleasantness, but I can see you ain't gonna budge. Looks like we're gonna find out what happens when an unstoppable force meets an unmovable object. Are you really sure Lawrence is worth it?" Marcus asked as he gestured to Karl and Steve once again.

Karl and Steve hauled Pablo up onto the bar and held him firmly in position. He struggled at first but it wasn't too difficult for them to subdue him.

"Now, are you sure you wanna do this? Last chance!" Marcus said.

"Fuck you!" Pablo growled as he spat in Marcus's face.

"Now that's just plain rude. But you got guts, old timer, I'll give you that," Marcus muttered as he recoiled backwards and wiped the saliva from off his cheek before resuming. "Alright, fine. They're your legs, buddy. Steve, proceed," he then instructed.

And so Steve began to strike empty bottles one by one off Pablo's knees. The pain was so overwhelming that Karl was forced to stuff a bar towel into Pablo's mouth just to muffle his screams. While Steve continued to whack bottle after bottle off Pablo, Marcus made his way over to an old dusty television set which was positioned above the bar.

"You know, it's funny. Well, not funny 'ha ha' as I'm sure you'll agree. Strange is maybe a better description, but the first few bottles hurt. I mean they really fucking hurt like a son-of-a-bitch. Not speaking from personal experience granted, but we're talking kneecaps caving in and turning to mush here, so it ain't exactly a stretch of the imagination. Anyway, the good news is you start to lose all feeling until eventually you really can't feel much of anything. It's the shock you see. The human body can only take so much pain before it overloads and shuts down. It varies from person to person of course but it's the body's way of dealing with high

99

levels of trauma. More often than not you simply pass out. But don't worry, we won't let you pass out on us. Wouldn't want you missing all the fun now, would we? Anyhow, I guess that's also when you know that you'll never walk again. Now don't be afraid to shout out the correct answer to the million-dollar question. You do this and we'll stop, but you have to co-operate. No? I ain't the one who's gonna spend the rest of their life in a wheelchair and sucking up their meals through a fucking straw. Hey, are you into baseball at all? I love it," Marcus continued as he turned on the television set and flicked a few channels to the baseball. The voice of the commentator following the game in the background also helped to blot out the noise of screams and smashing glass.

"Oh! That's an amazing strike right out of the park!" the commentator announced excitedly.

"And you have to wonder what it'll take to stop this young man, Chuck. He's on fire right now," Al, Chuck's co-commentator confirmed.

"That he is, Al. This guy is at the top of his game. Not only that but he's fast becoming a fans' favourite."

"Now don't you go passing out on me, old man. We got smelling salts, and just look at the mess your blood is making of my good friends' suits. You selfish bastard," Marcus said, avoiding the spray of claret.

"Strike two!" Chuck declared.

"And that one's heading for the stands. This guy is in a league all of his own."

"Right, I've had enough of beating this guy. My arm's getting tired. You take over, man," complained Steve.

"Really, Steve?" Marcus sighed.

"Yeah, I will say this though. It ain't like the movies. These glass bottles hold up pretty well. I thought we'd have way more smashed glass than this," Steve continued.

"That's cos they use sugar glass or some shit in the movies. This ain't the fucking movies, Steve! You might think that all this is pretty cool, but you gotta get your head in the game if you're truly serious about the work we do," Karl pointed out.

"I am! My idea to interrogate that last dude by rolling up a magazine and jamming it down his throat before pouring down a couple mouthfuls of bleach was an inspiration. We scared the shit outta that guy," Steve insisted.

"Yes, yes you did," Karl began, stopping only momentarily to sarcastically clap his hands slowly together. "But you also burned his fuckin' throat out. Even if he did know something he couldn't tell us squat after that, you twisted bastard. It's exactly that kind of shit I'm talking about. Yes, hurt somebody, but do it in such a way that you might actually obtain some useful information first. Anyway, you're right, Marcus. These bloodstains are ruining my jacket. We're talking quality Italian threads here too. And it's not as if I can take this shit to the dry cleaners," continued a rather distressed Karl as he dabbed rather optimistically at his suit with his handkerchief.

Just then in the background the sound of The Baseball Stadium Charge Organ Theme starts up and gets louder and louder, faster and faster, steadily building up. *"Do, do, do, do, do…"*

"Air… airpo… rt," Pablo muttered so faintly it was barely even a whisper.

"Do, do, do, do…"

"Shut the fuck up, you two! What was that? What did you say? Airport? Is that what you said?" Marcus asked, bending over Pablo.

"Yes. But you're too late," Pablo continued. He could take no more.

"That wasn't so hard, was it? See what you can achieve with the right incentives," Marcus said, just before shooting Pablo once in the head without so much as battling an eyelid.

"Did, diddla, did, da, da!" and at that very same moment the baseball anthem reached its climax.

"Want one?" Steve asked as he opened up his bag of cookies.

"Marcus just popped his head open like a ripe melon. I kinda lost my appetite."

"You ain't getting squeamish in your old age are you, Karl?" Steve sniggered.

"We're done here. Let's go," Marcus said, leading the way.

101

Chapter 12

Morgan and Stuart had woken up after a short sleep but were hitting new found levels of boredom. This worsened by the fact Morgan's iPhone had died long ago playing *Angry Birds* and *Candy Crush*. Now it seemed they'd exhausted everything else they could think of just to keep themselves amused, the inflight movies, radio, reading the airline magazine. They'd even studied the safety pamphlet. Admittedly a short read and mainly consisting of oddly unrealistic illustrations, but at least they were now experts and knew exactly what to do in an emergency situation. It had come to the point where the pair got out a piece of paper to play noughts and crosses. However, that could only last so long. Then it was the turn of hangman, which went well at first but ultimately uses up too much space on the paper.

"Ah spy wi ma little eye something beginning wi 'A'," Morgan began.

"Air hostess," Stuart murmured as he ogled at one.

"Oh bollocks. Right yer turn."

"Sorry? What are ay saying?" Stuart asked as he broke out of his smutty little world.

"'A'. Ya got my eye-spy word. Air hostess. Now it's yer turn."

Stuart thought for a second. "Wow! We're still playing that? Okay, eh? Ah spy wi ma little eye something… something… Ah really hate this game. Dae we huv tae play it?"

"Whatever." Morgan shrugged.

"God! Are we there yet? Sooo bored."

"We'll be coming in tae land soon," Morgan assured Stuart.

"Good. Ah need tae give ma legs ay proper stretch."

"Aye, ma legs are like jelly."

"Totally. Hey, Ah've just had a thought."

"Steady now. Remember what happened last time?"

"Ahh, sae funny. Not! No, Ah was just wondering about the movie *The Terminator*."

"Oh yeah, *The Terminator*," Morgan groaned.

"Well, if the psychotic robot had been successful in killing Sarah Connor, what then?" Stuart wondered.

"What then what?"

"What was his programming in such an eventuality? Was he tae carry on killing as many humans as possible before being stopped? Or was he meant tae get a job and try and integrate intae society? Or was he just destined tae end up in some grotty bedsit somewhere drinking himself tae oblivion while watching daytime T.V. until his power cells died?"

"Wow. A question for the ages there, Stuart. Ah dae sae look forward tae these random musings ay yers. That said, any thoughts on our situation?"

"Like?"

"Like what's our plan ay action is once we dae get tae where we're goin'?" Morgan then asked.

"Nae tae sure. What dae ya reckon?"

"Well, as we barely huv a dollar tae our names, Ah say we get the money. Then a hotel. Everything else we can play by ear Ah guess."

"Dinnae forget about Lawrence. We need tae find him tae, man."

Morgan peered out of the window. "Oh aye, ay course. An, eh? What about *The Rolling Stones* gig?"

"That's right. With aw this amazing stuff that's being happening Ah almost forgot about that. Ah reckon we could shoe horn it in. It's hardly a major detour. Lawrence would understand. He's rock n' roll for sure. It's practically on our way anyway," Stuart reasoned.

"Yer the boss."

"Hey, wouldn't it suck ass if we were tae crash now. Seriously, Ah mean everything's going too well. Something's gotta give," Stuart added.

"Aye, aye it would, Stu. And that's puttin' it mildly. It'd definitely put a major dampener on ma day. Ah'd actually rather no think about that possibility if it's aw the same tae ya. Yer the kinda guy who waits until yer having a great wee splash about in the sea in that before sayin' something about *Jaws*. An as soon as ya've got that theme tune in yer heid yer fun's deid."

"Sorry, it's just that here we are being propelled though the air at near the speed ay sound thousands ay feet above the earth in a wafer thin mental tube wi wings on. It's mental when yer stop and think about it. It defies rational thinking and logic. Fact is, it shouldnae even work. It's just no natural, man. We've absolutely nae business in the air. If it wasnae for the sheer brute force ay they six jet engines strapped either side ay us we'd be plummeting toward our Lord and maker doubled over screamin' blue murder wi our heids buried between our legs waiting tae kiss our arses goodbye."

"And if ye were fortunate enough tae somehow cheat death in a crash, chances are ye'd end up on some remote frozen mountain peak forced tae survive by turning tae cannibalism, like in that movie *Alive*. Which was a true story by the way. Either that or ye'd ditch in the ocean only tae end up as nothing more than glorified fish food. Ah mean, why give ya a safety belt? What the fuck is that for really? It's meant tae give ya the illusion ay safety, but really it's tae keep ya strapped tae yer seat sae they can identify whose bodies whose."

"Really?"

"Aye. And why give ya a life jacket? No much use if ya crash on land now, is it? Again, the illusion ay safety. Same reason ya get movies and meals. It's tae make everything appear normal like ye were sitting at home or out in a restaurant wi friends. If things dae go tits up what's the one thing ye dinnae get? A fucking parachute! Let's cut out the other shite and let ya take yer chances jumping out the back ay the plane. Probably tae expensive," Morgan mused, taking the conversation to the next level.

"Alright. Steady on there. Ah was just sayin'. Ye've gone tae far there," Stuart said, now feeling a little freaked out.

"Ye started it."

"We are now preparing for our descent into Dulles International Airport, Washington DC. Please remain seated with your seat belts fastened in preparation for landing and a member of our cabin crew will make sure your tables are fixed in their upright position. On behalf of everyone here at British Airways I'd like to thank you for flying with us and hope you will again soon," the pilot announced over the plane's intercom.

Five minutes later the plane approached the runway to land.

It had been at least an hour since Morgan and Stuart had arrived in Washington DC. They were sitting at a burger grill waiting on their connecting flight to California.

"Dae ya believe this shit?" Morgan exclaimed in horror.

"What?" Stuart garbled, his mouth more than full as he munched gleefully into his burger.

"Yuck! Ah've found yet another sodding gherkin in ma buggering burger! Ah hate those guys."

"No way. Ah didnae get ay single one. Ah love them tae. Weird," Stuart puzzled.

Morgan peeled the top off his bun to examine the full magnitude of gherkin infestation, "It's riddled wi them! Ah've obviously got yer one and ye've got mine, ya tit," he then concluded.

"Here, we'll swap," Stuart said, but it didn't stop him taking another big bite.

"Stop eating it then, fuck wit! No that it matters now. Ye've eaten half ay it already. Plus, it's covered in yer gob."

"Well, Ah'm aw outta ideas here dude," Stuart spat out in between bites.

"Also, small thing. But would ya please no talk wi yer mouth full. It's like watching a washing machine on spin cycle only somebody's left the door open. It's enough just eating ma own burger without unintentionally eating half ay yers as well," Morgan groaned.

Stuart took a long heavy slurp on his Sprite. "Oh, dry yer eyes, gay boy."

"Well, it's disgusting," Morgan insisted.

It didn't take Morgan too long to notice the man in black at the table across from theirs watching them intensely. Until then he'd successfully followed them all over the airport. The stranger had taken a seat by the door directly under a heater. He immediately wished that he hadn't as he was now beginning to sweat heavily. However, it was too late to move as he felt almost certain that Morgan had spotted him.

"Ah dinnae believe it! Dinnae look now but it's that creepy dude again from when we got on the plane. He's stalking us Ah tell ya," Morgan whispered.

105

What is it about people when you say something like "Don't look now but…" and what's the first thing they do?

Stuart looked straight back over his shoulder. "No him again. He's got a real boner for ya, Ah'll say that much."

"What's the matter wi ya, ya complete cock end? Ah told ya no tae look. Where's the difficulty in that?" despaired Morgan, incensed by Stuart's total lack of subtlety.

As Stuart started to ramble on about things they should do next Morgan continued to peep over at the man. As he did so he began to notice something very peculiar. Something that he couldn't fully explain. The guy's face started to contort almost as if it were melting away, and nobody else appeared to bear witness to it. Not even the man himself. Was this just Morgan's tired eyes playing tricks, or was his paranoia just getting the better of him? Maybe his foray into hallucinogenic drugs was coming back to haunt him in some kind of horrific acid flashback. Whichever way, Morgan had become transfixed.

"Jesus, Stuart. That weirdo's face is like peeling off or something. It's Si*lence ay the fuckin' Lambs* over there, dude!" Morgan said, as he signalled carefully in the stranger's direction.

Stuart did nothing. He wasn't making the same mistake twice.

"Well?" Morgan prompted.

"Dae Ah look or no?" Stuart stressed, overwhelmed by the seemingly contradictory nature of what Morgan had said and yet appeared to want him to do. The conflict in his mind was a form of mental torture.

"Aye, quick!" urged Morgan yet again.

"Where? What?" Stuart asked, but the man had vanished.

"Ah'm telling you he was just there," Morgan insisted.

"Is this jetlag? Yer acting kinda strange."

Once back on the plane Morgan still seemed a little unsettled.

"Ah dinnae see him. Ah think we're okay. Ah dinnae think he's followed us this time," Morgan assured himself.

"Who?"

"The nut job from the burger grill for God's sake!"

"Oh right, him. Nah, it's aw good… Wait, holy shit! There he is! Run! Run Ah tells ya! Run! Save yersel. Ah'll slow him down somehow. Go!" Stuart shrieked.

Morgan froze. "What the hell does he want?"

"Nothing. Ah'm kidding. He ain't even there. Just listen tae yersel. This is getting ridiculous."

"That's nae funny."

Stuart reached under his seat and produced a duty free bag. "Ah know, it's totally lame. Man up! Sae anyway, what did ya dae with yer share ay Lucus's money?" he then asked.

Morgan shook his head in disgust. "Whatcha mean, 'share'? Wait, ya sick bastard. Sae ya did take his money?"

"Well, yeah. Dinnae Ah no say this already?"

"Sae what did ya get?"

"Cigarettes and alcohol ay course. Just like one ay ma favourite *Oasis* songs, man."

"Yes, and why? We need that money."

"God, if Ah knew you'd react like this then Ah wouldnae huv bothered."

"Really? Ah told ya that Ah didnae want ya to take his money in the first place. Ya must've had a fair idea ay that. Just dinnae spend any more. Stu, are ya listening?" Morgan then asked, realising that Stuart seemed to have switched his focus.

"Oh, no. Nae again. Ah still think Ah got a wee bit ay the old gut rot," Stuart murmured, as he got up and moved quickly but tentatively in the direction of the toilet once again.

She looked at him. He looked at her. Morgan could barely believe it. As he turned his eyes met with the single most beautiful woman he'd even seen. She was stunningly gorgeous. Morgan didn't know what to do. He just hoped Stuart's diarrhoea was chronic. Morgan tried his utmost to look cool and calm. She looked at him and smiled, so Morgan casually reached into Stuart's bag and pulled out a magazine. He was looking at it but wasn't really 'looking' at it. The woman suddenly looked shocked and turned away. Morgan couldn't understand why so threw the magazine to one side, sighed and plugged in his earphones. Maybe he'd simply misread the signs.

A short while later Stuart returned. "Ah really hope that's the last of that. God, it burns. Ma poor wee arse is in tatters," he said as he sat gingerly back down.

"Aye, me tae. And please spare me the graphic details. Yer givin' me the boak here."

"Got any more ay that cream? Just tae cool the red raw burning and that."

"What cream?"

"That girlie moisturiser ay yers."

"Moisturiser? Ahhh! Ye've been using that on yer vile hairy hole? Jesus! Here, keep it!"

"Sound. Oh, aye. Had tae have a wee peek then, eh?" Stuart said, as he nudged Morgan and winked.

"What?" Morgan then smiled innocently before looking down at the magazine he'd just shown the world not to mention the woman of his dreams. "A porno? Ah'm gonna kill ya, ya dirty little perv!" he then continued angrily.

"Sorry. If Ah'd known ye'd be sae uptight about it Ah wouldn't have bought it. It's only bums, tits and fannies. Nakedness is nothing tae be ashamed ay," Stuart said, unable to appreciate the drama.

"There's nakedness and then there is nakedness. Ye really are quite the vulgarian. Honestly, Stuart, next ye'll be tellin' me ya brought some weed wi ya in aw… Err? Ya havenae brought any illegal substances wi ya though, huv ya?" Morgan then asked, realising that it wasn't an entirely impossible thing for Stuart to do.

Stuart paused for a moment. "Hardly," he replied, but wasn't at all convincing.

"Ya better no huv. Fuck's sake, Stuart, Ah'm no getting a full rectal examination on an account ay you. Ya might no mind getting the rubber glove treatment, but Ah dae!" Morgan emphasised, petrified at the very thought.

"Then dinnae worry. Although, why it's illegal in the first place is beyond me."

"And yet it is, Stuart, sae dinnae dae this tae me."

"Ah know. It's just sae stupid. Legalise the lot Ah say. And let's aw get high together. It'd be beautiful, man. Anyway, that's what Ah'd dae if Ah was in charge ay running things," Stuart insisted.

"Ya would say that. And if you were in charge we'd huv far more tae worry about than legalising yer habit," warned Morgan.

"Well, ya cannae say the supposed war on drugs is working, can ya? How can it be when half the world is shaped outta their box on a regular basis?"

"Ah dunno?"

"And it never will, no matter how much money they throw at it. Legalise it, tax it and ultimately control it. Aw ya can dae is put the literature out there and let people make up their own minds. It's meant tae be a free country, is it no? We go tae war over the protection ay our freedom and democracy, yet Ah cannae really dae what Ah want. No really. Ah ain't hurting anybody else. It's ma choice. Ma decision. How dare they say what Ah can an cannae dae. It's an invasion ay ma human rights, man."

"Well, Ah suppose they'd say yer funding crime and breeding the next generation ay junkies. Anyway, we've covered this a thousand times before. Yer just gonna get yersel worked up," Morgan said, realising that this was a path he'd rather not walk down. Especially on a crowded plane.

"No, Ah'm no. And that's bullshite. It's a problem that they're helpin' tae perpetuate. Ye'd more than half crime overnight if the government just had the bottle and foresight tae regulate and market it like cigarettes or booze, and tae be fair alcohol is by far and away the worst drug out there anyway. More people die ay alcohol related incidents than aw the other drugs combined. Christ, more people are addicted tae prescription drugs, but that's okay. More people die in motoring accidents for fuck's sake. But we dinnae ban cars. It just doesnae make sense tae me. It's complete double standards," Stuart argued.

"No the now, eh. Wind yer neck in," Morgan stressed, as he reached over and began to fumble around the back of Stuart's head and neck.

"What are ya dein'?" Stuart protested.

"Just checkin' tae see if ya come wi an off switch or some kinda mute button," Morgan explained, still very much embarrassed at Stuart's chosen topic of conversation and perhaps more importantly the level of volume at which he'd chosen to air it.

"What dae ya mean?"

"Look, Ah ain't disagreeing wi ya. That's just the way it is. Ah guess what Ah'm really tryin' tae tell ya is tae shut the hell up! Stop banging on about yer bloody love ay narcotics. Ah'm tae young and sexy tae go tae jail, man. Ah wouldnae stand ay chance. Those places are packed tae the rafters wi violent nutters and sexual deviants."

"Yeah, well maybe Ah dae huv a wee spliff's worth. What of it?" Stuart confessed like some kind of petulant child.

"What a cock! And the sad thing is Ah know yer no joking. Yer gonna get us arrested and deported. Right, just fuckin' leave me alone. Ah dinnae know ya if anybody asks. Ah cannae even look at ya right now, never mind talk tae ya," Morgan stewed.

"Bothered?"

Morgan and Stuart spent the rest of the journey apart from one another. As far as Stuart was concerned Morgan was being overly sensitive, so naturally wasn't taking him at all seriously. Instead he was looking at this as yet another minor and temporary fall out. That was the thing about Morgan and Stuart. They were always falling out over the most trivial of things, and at the time of any one of these arguments Morgan in particular would take whatever it was personally.

So there the two of them were exchanging moody glances, Morgan looking over every so often with a face like thunder, and Stuart waiting until the very second Morgan looked away before pulling a silly face.

Chapter 13

Lawrence was blissfully unaware of just how close to death he'd come. He only just managed to get out of Pablo's bar with minutes to spare, and he'd need every single one of those precious minutes because he wasn't out of danger yet. He was now on his way to the airport, but the only trouble was Marcus, Karl and Steve now knew he was headed there too. They'd never come so close. There was no way that they were going to let him slip through their fingers. It was vital that they caught up with him at the airport otherwise he could simply get on a plane and there was every chance they'd never see him again.

Lawrence arrived at the airport in good time. His flight left in a couple of hours. Nonetheless he had to work fast. After, all he had a few major changes to make to his appearance before he could leave as regards to his borrowed passport, so he headed straight for a rest room where he locked himself in a cubicle to start his transformation.

It didn't take long for the wolves to turn up looking for their prey.

"Where is that little maggot?" Marcus snarled as his eyes searched through the crowds.

"Right, we clearly ain't gonna find him this way. We should split up. Steve and I will check out the restaurants and shops, Marcus, head over and scope out the people queuing at the check-in and flight desks. Come on! Let's move," Karl said, the tone of urgency in his voice all too apparent.

Lawrence had all but finished his final alterations and there was still time to spare, so he put his things to one side and nipped over to a Starbucks for a coffee. Unfortunately, Steve recognised him, or rather Pablo. Perplexed at the sight of Pablo's apparent doppelganger he decided to pursue him to investigate further, so he followed him back to the rest room. When Lawrence went to close the cubicle door behind him he suddenly felt it being forced open from the opposite side.

"Err? Excuse me, buddy, but there's actually someone in here trying to take a piss! The nerve of some people. Shit, my shoes. Fuck's sake!" Lawrence yelled out before going on to accidentally urinate all over the tiled floor and his sneakers.

"I'm well aware of that fact, you fuck!" Steve acknowledged as he shoved his way into the cubicle and pulled out his gun.

"Please, don't kill me! What do you want? Money?" Lawrence squealed, wrongly believing that he was being mugged.

"I ain't robbing you jerk-ass! So keep your voice down or I will pop you, understand?"

"Okay, what do you want?"

"I'll tell you what I want, and that's for you to stop struggling. Do you want me to shoot you? Cos I will. You may very well be a slippery son-of-a-bitch, but I'm pretty confident that you can't outrun a bullet. Now, I want you to come withhhhh…" Steve began, but his legs shot out from under him before he could finish his sentence.

He'd slipped on Lawrence's urine and smashed his face off the rim of the toilet. There was blood everywhere. Steve had knocked out most of his front teeth and broken his nose but was still conscious, albeit barely. It was more than enough to make Lawrence's toes curl though. He hated the sight of blood yet he still had enough of his wits about him and was quick to seize the opportunity to grab Steve's pistol from off the floor. Steve just squirmed around on his hands and knees as he moaned unable to really front any kind of resistance. A mixture of concussion and shock had completely dazed him rendering him inert. He just didn't appear to know where he was.

"Don't you move! Who are you? What do you want from me, man?" Lawrence gasped, eager for answers now that he had the upper hand.

"Shit… Ahhh! Fuck me! Ahhh! I can't fuckin' breathe. I think you broke my nose, you fucking asshole! Oh my God, are they my teeth?" Steve murmured as he made a vain attempt to gather up some of his missing teeth.

"Well, they ain't mine. And I didn't do anything. You fucking slipped. Who the hell are you anyway Goddamn it? Wait, did Mr

Leony send you? Cos you can tell him from me that it was an accident, okay. That crazy old bitch started the fire, not me."

"Lawrence? I'll be, I'll be damned. It is you. I... I can't believe it's really... you. You, you lucky piece of shit," Steve said as he spat out more blood from his mouth in an attempt to clear his throat.

"The hell with you, you psycho. I'm outta here," Lawrence said as he pointed the gun at the back of Steve's head and began to position himself for a quick exit.

"I... just, ahhh! Want... want you to know that I enjoyed smashing that stubborn old bastard's kneecaps in."

"Excuse me?" Lawrence stopped dead in his tracks. He knew what Steve meant and his finger tightened on the trigger. Rage like he'd never known before began to course through his veins.

"Ahh, Ah! Pablo, we fucking killed him."

And with one muffed shot from his own suppressed pistol Steve was dead. Lawrence was stunned for a moment. He froze. Paralysed with fear he found himself unable to move. He'd never killed anyone before. Well, not deliberately at any rate. Not that he was sorry. It was surprisingly easy. However, he was now running on pure adrenaline.

His flight was due to leave. Lawrence quickly wiped the piss and blood from off his shoes before straightening himself out. He then tidied away his things and made his way directly to the plane. He managed to slip right past Marcus and Karl, more out of sheer dumb luck than anything else. He was clear of danger for now. The flight left on time and Lawrence was now on his way to Britain where he hoped to locate Stuart and more importantly the ticket.

Sure enough Lawrence found where Stuart was living, but not before he'd met their less than welcoming landlord. It was he who also told him about Morgan. This was a further messy complication, yet it was almost irrelevant as Lawrence began to suspect that they already had the winning lottery ticket. This was later confirmed when he found himself following Morgan and Stuart back to the airport.

Chapter 14

Lawrence didn't just kill Steve that afternoon in that airport toilet. His action had inadvertently given a faint-hearted old cleaner such a shock that he dropped dead on the spot from a massive heart attack. Being a busy airport toilet the bodies were soon discovered.

"Marcus, I found Steve," Karl said, his face ashen with horror and disbelief.

"Well, where the hell is he? Has he seen Lawrence?"

Karl pointed towards the toilet which by then was crawling with airport security. "The rest room. He's fucking dead."

"What? Dead? What do you mean, dead? How?"

"I didn't get a good look but his face was pretty smashed up. And you're not gonna believe this but I think he's been shot in the head."

"What? Holy fucking shit!" Marcus blurted out turning more than a few heads in the process.

Karl rubbed his forehead in frustration. "Maybe we underestimated out target."

"Bullshit! Steve was a goddamned professional. We are professionals."

"Then explain to me what's happening here, Marcus. Cos this is not the way things were meant to go down."

"He got lucky is all."

"Well, he's turning out to be a regular rabbit's foot. I do the killing. It's not meant to work the other way!"

"Hey, you know the hazards of this business as well as I do. Don't lose your nerve and start second guessing things now. As I said, he got lucky. But luck runs out," Marcus insisted.

"You better be right."

"Pass me over your cellular. I better tell Mr Leony before he sees this circus on *CNN* and realises what an absolute cluster fuck this whole operation has become."

"What are you gonna say?"

Before Marcus could respond Mr Leony answered the call. *"Marcus. Speak to me. I trust you've news."*

"Of a sort."

"What do you mean, 'of a sort'?"

"Well, we've located Lawrence."

Mr Leony's anger seemed to travel through Marcus's phone and slap him in the face, *"Well, halle-fucking-luja! What do you want? A fucking medal! So where the fuck is he?"*

Marcus looked at Karl in dreaded anticipation of the 'but' that was to follow. "But, well…"

"But fucking well what?"

"Well, we're at the airport. Problem is Lawrence managed to get on a plane."

"So you in fact don't have him? Correct?" Mr Leony then asked in a disturbingly calm tone.

"Correct."

"You know, for supposed professionals you ain't so professional! I mean I didn't realise it was amateur hour. Is it amateur hour?"

"No."

"THEN WHY ARE YOU WASTING MY TIME WITH THIS SHIT?!! You're like the Three Stooges. Total fuck ups! And this ain't my problem. It's yours!" Mr Leony blasted.

"Yeah well, we're two of three now."

"Two of three? What the fuck are you saying, Marcus?"

"Steve is K.I.A."

"What?"

"It's getting messy. Steve is dead. Looks like Lawrence killed him."

"I couldn't give a sweet fuck from the Virgin Mary herself. Maybe you'll work a little harder now that you have a personal stake in this fiasco too. Find him, gentlemen. And soon. My patience is running out. I'm this fucking close to bringing out a contract on you. Good day!" Mr Leony said before abruptly hanging up.

"So what did he say?" Karl asked.

Marcus passed Karl back his phone. "You mean you didn't hear? He's pissed off. What do you think? Listen, we need to find out which plane he got on."

"I doubt they'll tell you that."

"They fucking better."

They made their way over to the flight desk where Marcus flashed his fake F.B.I. badge at the woman behind the counter. "Agent Dyson and this is my partner Agent Sharp, F.B.I. We require your assistance and full co-operation in a case of the upmost importance," Marcus said as he removed his shades.

Was it a mountain of make-up or was there really a woman under there? It spoke. There must be. "Oh, my good gracious. Of course. I will assist in any way that I can. What seems to be the problem?" she then asked.

"Outstanding. This is a national security matter, mam. I must insist on your total discretion."

"Whatever you need, sir."

"We believe a particularly dangerous individual going by the name of Lawrence Lowmax departed from this airport not five minutes ago. Could you confirm this?"

The woman typed in the information into her computer. "I'm sorry. The last flight to leave was bound for the United Kingdom, and I'm afraid that name does not appear on the passenger manifest," she informed them.

"What? Gimme that!" Marcus snapped as he whipped the screen around and ran his finger down the list. "Pablo Santez? That fucking sneaky fuck!"

"What?" asked Karl.

"Well, either Lawrence grew fucking wings and flew outta here or Pablo's risen from the dead. Or, and I think this is the more likely option, Lawrence is using Pablo's name and a fake passport."

"Is that all, gentlemen?" the woman asked politely.

Marcus looked the woman up and down. "Actually no. Do you have a man in your life?"

"No, why?" the woman blushed.

"It's no surprise. Do us all a favour and wipe that repugnant shit from off your ugly fat face. You can't polish a turd so don't try. Let's go, Karl."

"Well I never!" the poor woman gasped as they walked away.

"Why is he going to the UK?" Karl wondered.

Marcus shook his head in despair. "I don't know. Maybe he's just running scared. He's gotta know that we're on to him now. My only worry now is that we may have lost him for good."

"So do we follow him?"

"Maybe. I dunno? I need to make a few calls first."

Chapter 15

Lawrence hated flying. He suffered quite a severe case of vertigo so he'd never normally purposefully go up in an aeroplane. After all, he didn't even have his own passport. He believed firmly in the 'if man was meant to fly then God would've given him wings' school of thought, but of course he had an almighty big carrot dangling in front of his nose as an added incentive. Yes, you're damn right he'd give it a good go for a shedload of cash, no matter what it took. So to overcome this phobia he kept that thought at the back of his mind and vast amounts of Valium everywhere else. It seemed to have the desired effect. However, Lawrence was taking enough of the stuff to sedate a baby elephant. And its mother. He was flying from the west coast of America to Britain and within a day or so of arriving was on his way back again so was spending many long hours under its influence. Lawrence also had to make sure he looked as much like Pablo's passport as humanly possible. Unfortunately, Lawrence had become so wasted that he just wasn't making his usual touch ups to his latex mask. It had come to the point where he was beginning to scare small children. At times he bore more resemblance to some kind of abstract oil painting. Even worse was his reckless decision to make actual contact with Morgan. It wouldn't have mattered too much as he was in disguise, but telling people about your drug induced visions is another matter altogether. It was amazing that he wasn't slapped into a restraint jacket and thrown into a padded cell, let alone granted permission to get on an aircraft. He was lucky that people thought he was nothing more than a dottled old man so instead helped him on his way. Lawrence had absolutely no recollection of getting on or off planes, only of waking up semi-straight in departure lounges. It was from there that he made his way to Stuart's flat before topping up on Valium again for the return journey home. When he arrived back in California he was absolutely wrecked, and when you also factor in the added effects of jet lag it was little wonder that he didn't know whether he was coming or going. Thankfully the Valium had begun to wear off so he knew he had to make some kind of attempt at getting his hands on that ticket. First however, he had to ditch his latex disguise. It was itching like hell.

Chapter 16

Marcus and Karl were back at Harvey's office. They were still reeling from the unexpected twist in events that had culminated in Steve's death. Marcus hadn't uttered a word in hours, he just stared blankly into space as he contemplated their next move. Karl and Harvey on the other hand were engaged in conversation. Not that Karl was in much of a talkative mood either, but Harvey had left him with little choice.

"Oh my God. I still can't believe that Steve is dead. Seriously, man," Harvey said, shaking his head in bewilderment.

Karl felt as if he'd lost a surrogate son or baby brother. Steve was like family to both him and Marcus.

"So you keep saying. Look, I can't deal with this right now. Okay? I really don't wanna discuss it," Karl said angrily, his temper already starting to fray.

"Yeah, I know but…"

"But nothing. Please, just let it go."

"Jesus, sorry. It's just that. Well, I was thinking maybe…"

"I don't care! Shut the fuck up, Harv! I don't know how else to say it. Talk about something, anything else. Just not this."

Harvey's mouth had already started to move before his brain had a chance to catch up. "I just don't get it. He was armed. How did that punk get the drop on him? And why did…"

"Do you want a smack in the mouth? Is that it? Cos I will. I mean that can be the only reason you seem to be purposely ignoring me and persisting with this annoying shit!" threatened Karl.

There was a short pause but it felt like an eternity to Harvey who by then just couldn't help himself. "Dead? God rest his soul. Poor bastard. What a waste. Sorry, you're right. Let's just leave it at that."

"Thank you."

"God, I just can't get over it."

"Yeah, well he's dead! Believe it! Get over it! End of fucking story!"

"Jesus, God. Sorry, man," apologised Harvey.

"What are you, a religious nut or something all of a sudden?"

Harvey was a little taken aback. "What do you mean by that?"

"I mean, what's with all the Jesus, God talk? And God rest his soul bullshit? What, have you found the Lord? Are you some sort of born again Christian or something like that? Cos that's how you sound. Knock that crap off!"

"Well, I do believe in God if that's what you're getting at. Look, I had a lot of time to think about things while I was in jail. It kinda put things into perspective."

"I might've fucking guessed. I hope you're getting all this, Marcus. And that's the best you could do with your time inside was it? Not study for a degree in something useful?" Karl sneered as he sipped at his coffee.

"So fucking what if I do? Plenty of people do, you know. In fact, most of the world believes in a God of some kind or other."

"Yeah, more's the pity. I sure as hell don't. And there's plenty of people nowadays with their eyes open to reality who would agree with me when I said this God thing is a pile of garbage. I mean, most of the world's conflicts and wars have their foundations in religion. You've a country or group of people who believe in one thing and another who believe in something else. It's a 'my gang's' better than 'your gang' kinda mentality. Next thing you know they're trying to kill each other over it to prove their particular brand of bullshit is superior to the other. It's so divisive. There's nothing good or pure about war, between human greed and the colour of people's skins. It's gotta be the number one killer. Just as any God would want I'm sure," Karl said scathingly.

Harvey added a little more sugar to his own coffee. "That's a bit rich coming from someone who kills people for a living. Besides, I was brought up in a religious household and it didn't do me any harm," he argued.

"Pot, kettle, black. You're no saint either. So I'd say that's highly debatable. What's your fate gonna be come judgement day I wonder? And I'm not the one sitting here pretending to be something I ain't."

"I'm just saying. I know I've made mistakes. I ain't perfect. I'm well aware of that fact. But then who is? It's part of being human and that's what the bible tries to show us. How to be a better person. Anyway, I don't do that shit no more, remember?"

"That's alright then. Come on in. Welcome to paradise. Take your rightful place at God's side. And the only reason you ain't still doing what I do is cos you were caught," Karl said sarcastically.

"Maybe that was God's will all along."

"God's will? That's handy."

"Jesus Christ. You know what? Fuck you, man. What I do or don't believe in is none of your damned business."

"Blaspheming now? I'm shocked. And yes, I absolutely agree it is your business. The problem there is most religions do not stick to that principle. It's all about the hard sell. Believe what I believe or you're going to hell or you're in some way not worthy. You said you were brought up in a religious household. I put it to you, is that fair? I believe in the right to choose. Perhaps that's been taken away from you. Do you ever think about that? Shouldn't you be left to form your own opinion?" Karl reasoned.

"I have made up my own mind!" Harvey insisted.

"Was it not Aristotle who said, 'give me a child until he is seven and I will show you the man'. That's a pretty ace piece of philosophising if you ask my humble opinion. Have you really made up your own mind? You just admitted it's what you grew up with. I'd call that brainwashing."

"That's crazy."

"Is it? Come on, the bible is nothing more than an over-romanticised fairy tale, is it not? No different than Santa Claus or the fucking tooth fairy. Not only that but there's not one single piece of hard evidence to back the whole thing up in the first place. Now that's crazy."

"Jesus was real. Santa Claus and the tooth fairy? Come on. What kind of argument is that? They're pure fantasy. Kid's stuff."

"Other than the bible there's no hard evidence that Jesus existed either. Isn't it strange that one of the most famous figures in history ever has never had a mention or been documented anywhere else? At least even once. I mean, that kind of shit generally doesn't go unnoticed."

"Whatever."

"Have we not evolved beyond all that? I'm talking science here. Darwin's theory of evolution. We used to believe the world was flat and that Adam and Eve were the first people on earth for crying out loud. But whoops, what's this? I've just found a dinosaur bone. We know so much more than we've ever known before, but no, let's ignore all that in favour of some cock and bull story. Some people would call that denial," Karl continued.

"Look, some things transcend reason and logic. It's about faith," Harvey maintained.

"Are you fucking serious? Listen to yourself. Imagine I'd just come up with the bible yesterday. Nobody had ever heard of it before. It's a brand new concept. But I can't prove it in any way. Instead I just insist that you have faith that it's all true. How convenient can you get? I mean, that's one hell of a clause to stick in the contract, ain't it? You'd be labelled a madman and rightly so. I could tell you that there's a highly evolved race of aquatic cocker spaniels living at the bottom of the ocean handing out free brochures to far-flung exotic destinations that don't actually exist. But that doesn't necessarily make it fucking so."

"Highly evolved aquatic cocker spaniels?"

"Yeah, I dunno where that came from?"

"I should say."

"What I'm saying is if the bible were taken to a court of law as a character witness to a crime it'd be thrown out before it even had a chance to sit down. It has no credibility."

"Yeah, and don't forget who you swear an oath to before you sit down."

"Don't remind me. I do appreciate the irony," Karl conceded.

"Anyway, I'm not saying you take everything literally. That's the Old Testament and creationism you're talking about."

"Of course not. That'd be nuts. What part of the bible are we on now? You said it yourself. Old Testament? New Testament? It's been rewritten so many times I forget. It's like a bad movie remake. Sure, the original was a fantastic yarn, but that's all it ever was, not deserved of a sequel, and certainly not worth retelling with better special effects and a bigger budget. And that's what all these religions are anyway. Rehashed diluted reboot versions of the same story. Whatever bits that just happen to appeal at any given time. And if it's really the word of God why change it at all?"

"Well, science can't tell you everything. There are some things we just can't explain and that go way beyond our comprehension."

"Absolutely, but at least it's trying. And just cos we can't explain something doesn't mean we just fill in the blanks with whatever we like the sound of. Besides, religion was as much a tool of control as anything else. A way to rule and manipulate the masses. We've got television and the Internet for that now, not to mention it's a way to explain our own mortality and general fear of death. In fact, I'd go as far as to say the whole human race has basically got delusions of grandeur. Collectively we're all jumped up egomaniacs convinced in our own self-importance. How arrogant are we to assume we're any more important than the family dog? We're only separated by a few strands of DNA, or maybe the survival instinct is so strong that we're willing to believe anything rather than accept our own end."

At that moment Marcus's phone began to ring. It was his contact from passport control at the airport. *"Marcus?"*

"Yeah!" he replied snapping out of his trance.

The voice continued. *"You wanted me to tell you if that name turned up again."*

"Yeah!"

"Well, it has. Pablo Santez's plane will be coming in to land in the next couple hours."

"Are you certain?"

"There's no doubt about it. I'll consider your favour cashed in. We're even. See you around, Marcus."

Karl hadn't finished there. "Look, believe what you wanna believe I guess. Whether that's Christ, Buddha, the Prophet Mohammed, Allah or fucking Elvis, I really couldn't give a fuck. What I do take exception to is people trying to force their beliefs on me. That's really where things get messy. If people could just accept and in fact celebrate we're all different then things would be cool. After all, it would be a pretty boring place if we were all the same. But we just can't, can we? Surely if you were that secure in whatever you believed in it wouldn't matter what anybody else believed. You'd just sit there quietly smug that you'd picked the right one, and the way I see it is this. They can't all be right, but they sure as hell can all be wrong."

"I wasn't preaching but okay. What about morals?" Harvey asked.

"What about them?"

"I believe in them."

Karl shook his head. "Morals are just what's right. Common sense and decency should tell you that."

"It's the cornerstone of our civilisation as we know it, formed from religion."

"Fine, take them and throw away the toxic dressing. Anyway, you've broken most of them yourself, dumbass. As have I. And you're not the only one, you hypocritical bastard. Civilisation? We're just a fuel or food crisis away from total anarchy. Then you'll see just how civilised we really are. Trust me, if push comes to shove we'd turn on each other like animals."

"Well, I take great solace in that there's something better after all this," Harvey insisted.

"You were born with you own mind. Use it. You shouldn't need the bible or any other religion to use as a crutch through life. I thought you were stronger than that. Live this life, don't pin all your hopes on some utopian afterlife. This may be all you get."

"What do you make of all this, Marcus?" Harvey then asked as he turned to face him.

"I don't have an opinion on this shit right now. I've bigger fish to fry. Besides, never talk politics or religion, it's a recipe for fall out. To be honest I'm still giddy from the whole Santa, tooth fairy is nothing but fantasy bombshell. But F.Y.I. the best bit of the bible is when they enter the Matrix and Darth Vader tells Luke Skywalker that he's really his father before they finally destroy the ring in the fires of Mordor and eventually return home to Hogwarts for a game of fucking quidditch," Marcus said, unexpectedly lightening the mood.

"Holy shit! Was that a joke? You never joke," Karl gasped, before bursting into laughter.

"I have my moments. Anyway, enough of this goofing around, you pair of whining bitches. It's time to get our game faces on. That

125

was the phone call I had been counting on. Get your shit together, Karl. Pablo, I mean Lawrence, or whoever the fuck he is has resurfaced."

"Can I come?" asked Harvey.

"No, you stay here in case anything goes wrong," Marcus ordered.

"You can't come, remember? What we're doing is immoral," Karl smirked. He just had to have the last word.

With that Karl and Marcus moved out and made their way back to the airport in the hope they would catch up with Lawrence. When they arrived they waited by the entrance to watch out for him.

"Do you see him yet?" asked Karl.

Marcus looked around. "No, but I do see Pablo or somebody who looks exactly like him. What the fuck is going on here?"

"It can't be him. You shot him dead!"

"Don't you think I don't know that, Karl? Could Pablo have a twin we didn't know about? I dunno? Maybe Pablo double crossed us and sent us on a wild goose chase giving Lawrence time to slip off in a different direction."

"Then who killed Steve?"

"I dunno?" Marcus sighed.

"Well, if that ain't Pablo or Lawrence who the fuck is it? I mean, could it be a disguise of some kind?"

"I dunno? Maybe. If it is it's an impressive one."

"So what now?"

"The only thing we can do. Let's tail him and find out what the fuck he's up to. This guy is the only lead we have," Marcus surmised, the seeds of doubt now weighing heavy in his mind.

Chapter 17

Now firmly back on terra firma Morgan and Stuart made their way out of the airport.

"Finally we're here. Ah've had it wi airports. Ah cannae wait tae get tae the hotel and huv a nice long steaming hot shower and chill out," Stuart admitted.

"Ya said it, mate. Wait... look, Stuart. Yellow taxi cabs. Just like the ones ya see in the movies. Cool. Hey, taxi!" Morgan yelled as he flagged one down and got in.

"Yo! Where to, fellas?" asked the cabbie.

"The Hilton please," Morgan answered enthusiastically.

"Sure thing, buddy."

Stuart began to rummage around inside his bag to retrieve his shades. "Ahh, that's more like it. What dae ya think? Sweet, eh?"

"When did ya get those? Did ya get me a pair?" Morgan then asked.

"Ye've got something even better, dude. Something special. Check out this bad boy."

"It's a sun visor cap?" Morgan said. He couldn't hide his disappointment.

"No just any sun visor cap. No, sir. It has a built in fan and radio. But that's no even the best bit. It has beer dispensers. See, ya can huv two tins ay lager either side ay yer heid. Then ya just suck on the straw at the side there thus gettin' an instant icy cold refreshing mouthful ay the golden nectar while on the move whenever ya desire. It's pure magic, eh?" Stuart revealed as he gleefully presented Morgan with his gift.

"Oh yeah. Top-ay-the-fucking-pops, man. Cool, expensive designer Oakley shades vs tacky dayglow 'look at me Ah'm a tourist please mug me' shite. Score. It's nae contest. Ah dinnae at aw feel like a prize tit. Cheers, Stu." Morgan sighed as Stuart wrestled the monstrosity onto his head.

"Dinnae mention it, bud. Ah knew ye'd love it."

"Say, where are you boys from? That's quite the accent you have there. You on vacation?" the cab driver then asked.

"Scotland. And aye, kinda," Morgan answered.

The taxi driver nodded in acknowledgement. "Oh yeah. Awesome. You're Scotch. I have relations from over your side of the pond. From London. The home of haggis. They love wearing those crazy tartan skirts there too, ah? Like that movie *Braveheart*. Freedom!" he then cried.

"Riiiight. Ah think ye've got a few things a wee bit mixed up there."

"Oh really? Like what?"

"Well, most of it. They're kilts, no skirts. Scotch is a whisky. Haggis is a Scottish delicacy. And London is actually the capital city ay England. It's like a whole other country, which would make yer relations English," Morgan pointed out.

"Sorry about that. I forget you Scotch and English don't get on, do you? And now I think about it my relations are from Ireland."

"Sae they're Irish then? And just sae ya know *Braveheart* is largely a fictitious story loosely based on historical events. We actually get on pretty well these days," Morgan continued.

"Excellent. As a great American once said, 'give peace a chance'."

"That was John Lennon."

"Exactly. *Led Zeppelin* kicked ass, man. And I've gotta say your English is very good," the cabbie chuckled, oblivious to his errors.

"Yeah, okay," Morgan smirked as he looked over to Stuart.

Lawrence was by now in hot pursuit. "Follow that cab!" he cried pointing frantically in the direction of Morgan and Stuart's departing taxi.

The cab driver looked back at Lawrence in his rear-view mirror. "I've been waiting my while life to hear those words. Better buckle up, partner!"

"What words? Why? Wow! Slow down, dude! I said follow, I said nothing about breaking the sound barrier. Or my neck for that matter. I've managed to stay alive this long, I don't wanna die here with you now!" Lawrence yelled as he held on for dear life.

As the driver swerved erratically in and out traffic he continued their conversation. "This is great! What are you, a cop? F.B.I. maybe? Can I see your badge cos I was going to be a cop you know? But I failed the medical. It's bullshit though! Okay, I've put on a few pounds. So what? It's discrimination, man. I dunno? Perhaps you could put in a good word for me. So are you undercover? What's the case?" he then asked, bombarding Lawrence with question after question.

"What? No to all the above! And stop looking at me! Keep your eyes on the road for Christ's sake!" Lawrence begged as he pointed to the busy road ahead.

"Gotcha. Mum's the word. I won't blow your cover." he then winked knowingly.

"Goddamn! He's in a hurry. Do you think we've been made?" asked Karl as he watched Lawrence's cab disappear into the distance in a cloud of burning rubber.

Marcus flagged down a cab pushing a family to one side in the process. "Maybe, but I don't see how. Come on get in!"

"What about the Jeep?"

"It's back there. We've gotta move now."

They both entered the taxi then bellowed in unison, "Follow that cab!"

"Are you taking the piss? Get the fuck outta my cab, you pair of clowns!" snarled a less than impressed driver.

They both simultaneously flashed their badges and guns. "F.B.I.! Follow now!"

When all three parties arrived at the Hilton each booked into their own separate rooms. That same day Morgan and Stuart anonymously collected a cheque for around one hundred million dollars, most of which was deposited straight into Stuart's bank account for safe keeping. Some they exchanged for hard cash, something in the region of fifty thousand dollars in what Stuart referred to as 'carrying around funds'. They then placed said money into one of the hotel's very own burgundy suitcases purchased from the gift shop next to reception. It was from here that they planned to locate Lawrence and pay his bail.

Lawrence now knew they had the money and so decided there was nothing to stop him introducing himself. He'd kept a low profile long enough so he made his way to their room that same night wearing his latex mask so that he could explain in part the truth. Marcus and Karl waited for Lawrence to leave his room before they in turn followed him.

"STUART! Ye utter and complete bastard! Dinnae ye no think that joke has run its course? Would ye please, for the last time, stop covering the shower tray wi shampoo? It's dangerous. It's like a fuckin' ice rink in there. Ah was damn near doin' Bolero. Are ye tryin' tae kill me or what? Ah mean at best Ah could break an arm or a leg. At worst Ah could pop ma nut sack!" Morgan whimpered, nursing his rear and nether regions as he joined Stuart.

"Ah'm sorry, Morgan. It willnae happen again. It was meant tae be symbolic. Kinda like marking the end ay one life and the start ay another. One ay extreme wealth and decadence. WE SHALL LIVE LIKE KINGS!" Stuart cried out as he began to sing and dance around their opulent penthouse in total delirious abandonment.

"Ah dinnae think its sunk in yet. Oh, wait. No, there it is. WOOHOO! Who's got the money? That's right, ma friend, we got the money! I mean, look at this place. It's bigger than our whole flat. This changes everything. We can go anywhere. Do anything. The sky's the limit. Come on, let's start by raiding the shit outta the mini bar!" Morgan cheered as he joined in on Stuart's giddy celebration.

Moments later there was a knock at the door. "Oh, yeah. That'll be room service. Be a good chap and answer it would ya?" Stuart asked.

Morgan moved towards the door. "Ah certainly will, ma good man. In fact, it'd be ma pleasure."

It was all too much for Morgan. He hadn't eaten or slept properly in days, and to top it all off had just become a multi-millionaire. So perhaps it wasn't too surprising that he wasn't quite feeling his true self. When he opened the door only to be greeted by the man in black and his now quite hideous and very plastic-looking face he crumpled to the floor in a heap.

Stuart was quick to scoop Morgan up and rest him on a chair by the door. "What the bloody hell dae ya want, dude? Stop following

130

us! This has gone way too far. It's weird. Leave us alone or Ah'm gonna call security. Ah mean it!" he warned the stranger.

Just down the hall Marcus and Karl watched as the Pablo character entered the penthouse.

"There he is. What's he up to? And where the hell is Lawrence?" Karl said as he peered around the elevator door.

"I don't know. Maybe he'll lead us straight to him. He can't be too far away. This can't be a coincidence. Anyway, this shit has gone on long enough. It's time we go introduce ourselves and put an end to this fucking thing," Marcus said, as he carefully released the safety catch on his pistol.

"Wait, can I come in?" Lawrence asked as he entered the room and shut the door.

"Err? No, no you can't. Who do you think you are?" Stuart asked as he tried to usher him back towards the door again.

But before he had a chance to do so Lawrence suddenly ripped off his mask much to Stuart's horror. "It's me, Lawrence," he then announced as he revealed his true identity.

"AHHH! WOW! What the absolute fuck?!" Stuart screamed, almost jumping outta his own skin.

"I'm your uncle."

"Stuart took an unsteady step back. "B... b... but, but you're black?"

"So what? That's a bit racist, ain't it? You ain't a racist are you?"

"No. That's not what I meant at all. It's just that ma da was white and sae was his brother. Ah've seen photos ay them as kids. It's a family thing. Sae unless ye've done a reverse Michael Jackson Ah fail tae see how that's even possible. Besides, yer meant tae be in jail," Stuart pointed out as he desperately tried to figure out what was happening.

This just angered Lawrence. "Shit! Look, where's my fucking money?"

"Yer money? Ah dinnae think sae, pal."

Seconds later the door thundered open behind them and before they knew it they both had guns pointed directly at their heads.

"Lawrence? Where did you crawl out from under? Well, who cares. We got you now, you lowlife motherfucker!" Marcus yelled.

"And you're gonna pay big time for what you did to Steve," Karl added.

"Who the fuck is Steve?" Lawrence asked nervously.

"The guy you killed at the fucking airport! Ring any bells?" replied Karl angrily.

"Hey, that was an accident," insisted Lawrence.

"My ass it was! You fucked his shit up pretty bad then you shot him in the back of the head. How the fuck did you accidentally manage that?" fumed Marcus.

"Err? Ye know each other? What are ye guys, cops? Cos if ye are, then please arrest this guy. He's claimin' tae be my uncle and he's also tryin' tae rob me," Stuart said, taking the focus off Lawrence.

"Shut your fucking hole! We're not cops? And who the hell are you and how do you relate to this fucking mess?" Marcus snapped as he kept his gun pointed at Lawrence.

"Ah dinnae. Ah'm just Stuart. From Scotland," Stuart said nervously as he raised his hands in the air.

"Well, Stuart from Scotland, we're hired killers. What's his problem?" Marcus then asked as he walked over to Morgan who by then was beginning to come around again.

"He's wi me. Ah'm sorry, what? Hired killers?"

"What are you a couple of queers? And how the fuck can he be your uncle?" Karl asked.

"No! And that's what Ah said. Ah dinnae know who he is. But wait a second. You're hired killers?"

"Yes! Now shut up! This shit is confusing enough. The only thing I believe right now is that you're Scottish. Cos I can't understand half of what you're fucking saying. That's one messed up accent you got there!" barked Karl.

Morgan had by then woken up dazed and confused. "Ohh, what? What's going on? Who... who are you guys?" he then murmured.

"Go back to sleep, pal," Marcus said, as he cracked Morgan over the head with his gun knocking him out cold.

"NOOO! Morgan? Please don't! You'll hurt him!" Stuart stressed as he tried to make a tentative step towards his friend.

Karl quickly redirected his pistol towards Stuart. "Hey, stay where you are, dipshit! Where's the other guy? The Mexican?"

"Who? Mexican? What the hell is this? Is this some kinda twisted joke? Wait, are we on T.V.?" Stuart asked, now completely clueless as to what was going on, his eyes searching the room for evidence of hidden cameras in the vain hope that's all this was.

"Don't play dumb! The Pablo lookalike," Karl continued.

Lawrence realised that they hadn't yet figured out he was the Mexican. "Oh, him. He's in the rest room taking a leak," he then lied.

"The rest room? Check it out, Karl. I got 'em covered. Just watch your six. No more surprises, ah," Marcus directed.

Karl left the front room to investigate further. As he left room service arrived and there was a knock at the door.

"Expecting anyone?" Marcus asked as he backed slowly towards the door.

"Ah, it could be room service," Stuart replied.

"You better not be fucking with me," Marcus said as he kept his gun pointed back into the room and popped his head around the door. "Yeah, what?" he then asked.

"Your strawberry shakes and French fries, sir," the bellboy said as he lifted the lid on his silver tray.

Lawrence saw his opportunity. He dived at Marcus whose gun went off shooting the bellboy in the leg before, in the struggle to the floor, it went off again with deadly effect. Marcus was dead. Karl, who heard the shots, came running back through firing his gun at the only person standing at the time, Stuart, who still had his hands in the air screaming, "Don't shoot! Please don't shoot!" However, it was too late. Karl had shot him twice in the chest. This warned Lawrence who managed to return fire with Marcus's pistol killing Karl outright. It was a massacre and was over in seconds. There were bloody bodies everywhere, either dead or in pain. Morgan had by then started to come around once again, groggy and shaking.

"Ahhh, what? What's going on?" he asked Lawrence who he'd never set eyes on before.

Lawrence pointed his gun at Morgan. "Where's my fucking money, asshole? I don't wanna have to shoot you!"

133

"Ahhh! Ma head. Shit. Where's Stuart?"

Lawrence looked over his shoulder to where Stuart's lifeless body lay. "I'm sorry. Really I am. He's dead. They're all fucking dead!"

What Lawrence said didn't seem to register at first. Morgan was in autopilot as he stood up and made his way over to Stuart's position.

"Stuart, man. Get up. Stop messing around. Who are these people? What's going on? Stuart?" he slurred as he tried to gather himself.

"He's gone."

It took another moment before the realisation of what had happened clicked into place. When it did it knocked the wind out of Morgan like a punch to the guts. His knees just buckled as he fell to the floor in disbelief.

"Where's the damned money, asshole? I don't have much time!" yelled Lawrence.

"Who are you? What have you done?" Morgan sobbed.

"MONEY!"

Morgan pointed over to where the suitcase sat under the table. Lawrence checked it. He'd never seen so much money and it was so heavy he could barely carry it.

"Where's the rest?"

"We banked it. What do you think? All the account details are in the case with the money. Just take it and go!"

"Fuck! Right, I'm sorry to have to do this," Lawrence then said as he whacked Morgan over the top of the head knocking him out yet again before making good his escape.

For Morgan there followed a few days of intense and very confusing police questioning, everything he knew and all of which was confirmed, thanks in no small part to the only real eye witness. The bellboy, whose account of what happened along with the ballistics report of shots fired, verified almost everything. Morgan was later cleared of any wrongdoing but was asked to leave the country which he was more than happy to do.

Chapter 18

Turns out that Lawrence headed straight for the airport and got on the first available flight. He now found himself bound for Australia. The only problem was he wasn't allowed to take his huge burgundy suitcase on board as carry-on for the simple reason that he barely could. So he had little choice, despite his bitter protests, but to let it go in the hold along with the rest of the luggage.

"You must let me take it on board with me. You don't understand. Please. Come on Goddamn it!" Lawrence pleaded, making quite the scene at the check-in desk.

"This is not hand luggage, sir. So either the case goes in the hold or you don't get on the flight. It's the rules. I assure you it'll be perfectly safe there," the head of airport security explained.

"I don't believe this shit! Okay, but you better look after it. God, this is unbelievable," Lawrence said as he grudgingly gave over the case.

It was however improperly tagged and was duly misplaced so it was returned to the Hilton hotel as addressed. Not only that but Lawrence got to meet an old friend who was also travelling first class to Australia on business. It was none other than Mr Leony!

"Lawrence? Why don't you take a seat next to me? We have much to discuss you and I," Mr Leony said as he forcibly grabbed Lawrence by the shoulder.

"Mr Leony? Shit!" Lawrence cringed.

"Indeed."

This unfortunate turn of events was nothing compared to his horror when that same flight was hijacked by Jihadi Freedom Fighters who demanded the plane was redirected to Baghdad.

"WE ARE NOW IN CONTROL OF THIS FLIGHT! ANYONE WHO MOVES WILL BE SHOT!" one terrorist cried out as three others burst up from their seats waving custom made plastic automatic machine guns around erratically.

Neither Lawrence nor Mr Leony have ever been seen or heard of since. Interestingly though, everyone else aboard the flight were later rescued in a daring midnight raid executed perfectly by the S.A.S.

Chapter 19

Detective Williamson and Detective Parker were in Glasgow hospital's autopsy examination room where they had been waiting for the coroner's final verdict on the cause of Mr Raymond Lucus's death.

"Well, was it murder or no?" Williamson yawned as he glanced down at his watch.

"It willnae be long now," Parker said as he looked on fascinated by what he was seeing.

The coroner delved and poked around inside Raymond's throat making various tiny incisions but with very little luck. Williamson stood well back with his hand over his mouth. He wasn't nearly as enthralled by the experience as Parker. The smell was overpowering.

"Ah dinnae know. It's a bit ay a mystery. Although, Ah'm almost certain that we can rule out strangulation. The pressure marks around the neck area just aren't consistently severe enough to bring on asphyxiation. However, his brain was starved of oxygen. My guess is he choked. But why and on what? Oh, hello! Wait, there's the perpetrator," the coroner exclaimed as he pulled out something on the end of his tongs. He'd found the chunk of toenail which had lodged in Raymond's throat.

"What? Is that a toenail?" wondered Parker.

"Ye mean tae tell me that dirty stupid fat twat managed tae kill himself choking on his own toenail? Ah dinnae believe it. What a fantastic end tae ma career this has turned out tae be. Fuck's sake!" Williamson moaned bitterly.

"Aye, if this job has taught me anything at all it's to expect the unexpected." Parker nodded, "Ah just wish we coulda kept a lid on things for a little longer. Ah still dinnae quite know how the press picked up on this sae quick. No that it matters now." he then sighed.

The news report read. . . *"with the Prime Minister insisting that they will continue to work closely with their American counterparts, claiming that anything less would only be playing directly into the hands of terror. And to this end special emergency funds will be set aside in their continuing war against fanatical extremists. . .In other news, police are now categorically ruling out murder in the Mr Raymond Lucus case. Stating that it was an accident and his injuries were entirely self inflicted. It's unclear as to exactly what this means but it appears that the investigation is over and it's now case closed. . .I'm Bob Sanders, Sky news. And here's John McNamara with all the latest sporting action and results."*

Chapter 20

On the fourth day Morgan made his way back to the hotel to pick up his belongings. He'd arrived in America with nothing and was leaving with even less. His American dream had turned out to be more of an American nightmare. Their little trip was nothing short of a complete disaster and he knew that the flight back could never be as adventurous as the one over. Perhaps that was just as well given the circumstances. However, that was of little consolation to Morgan who'd been left absolutely devastated. He'd lost his best friend and was going to miss his immensely. It was something he'd probably never get over.

On leaving the hotel's reception he was stopped in his tracks. The manager had recognised him from earlier. "Excuse me, sir. I just wanted to pass on my condolences. Awful business. Simply awful," he said.

"Thank you. Ah just wanna get home."

"Of course. Oh, one more thing before you go. I believe that this belongs to you," he continued as he pointed to the burgundy suitcase. The case full of money!

"How did you get this?" Morgan stuttered, utterly shocked to see it again.

"I believe it was redirected here after it got lost at the airport. I received a call from the airport's lost and found department this morning. My brother works there you see, and I figured after everything you've been though I should do my best to get it back. You're lucky you put your things in one of our cases. That's the main reason it ended up back here and wasn't destroyed. I knew straight away it was yours as hardly anyone actually ever buys one of those hideous things."

"Really?"

"I know. I don't get why we keep stocking them. They're a total sales flop."

"No, Ah meant. Really?"

"Oh, right. I know. It's weird. It sure is heavy. What's in it? Gold bars or something," the manager giggled.

"Something like that." Morgan smiled as he turned to leave.

As he stepped into the revolving door at the hotel's entrance he began to spin wildly round and round for what felt like an eternity. He was then thrown into a short stumble and was then hit by a sudden dazzling light as he exited the building. It was so bright that he was forced to close his eyes. He felt so hot and disorientated that he lost all bearings. Morgan knew he'd fallen and was out flat on the ground but there wasn't anything he could do about it. When he tried to open his eyes to look up he saw the silhouette of something in front of him. He rubbed his eyes to try and clear his vision. It appeared to be the hazy outline of a figure dressed in brilliant white and bathed in a strange luminous aura. He rubbed his eyes once again but this time could feel the right side and then the left side of his face being gently smacked before the faint murmur of a friendly voice.

"Morgan, man. Ye okay?" uttered the familiar voice.

"Stuart?" Morgan mumbled. But how? It couldn't be.

"Morgan, snap outta it, dude," the voice continued, as Morgan's sight began to return fully.

"Stuart! Is it really you?" Morgan gasped as he looked Stuart straight in the eye.

"Aye, soppy bollocks. Who were ya expecting? Are ya okay, amigo? Ye've been passed out for about an hour or so."

"Err? How the hell? Ah thought ya were deid."

"Deid? What? It's you that's been out cold."

Morgan threw his arms around Stuart's neck, "Thank God!"

"Alright. Steady on, gay boy," Stuart sniggered, but couldn't break Morgan's embrace.

"Ya wouldnae believe the nightmare Ah've just had by the way. It was totally mental!" Morgan said as he got to his feet and looked around to the all too familiar surroundings of their filthy little flat.

"Ah bet. Ye were trippin' outta yer box, man. Ah told ya tae go easy on that skunk. It's potent as fuck. Ya just had the whitey tae end aw whities," Stuart explained.

"Really? Holy shit. That was crazy." Morgan sighed with relief.

"Anyway, huv Ah got some totally amazin' news tae tell ya. Ah nearly forgot thanks tae all yer antics. Ye better sit down," Stuart said excitedly.

"What?"

"AH WON THE LOTTERY, MORGAN!"

THE END?